# WHY ME?

Other Apple paperbacks you will enjoy:

*One Step at a Time*
by Deborah Kent

*Nobody Listens to Me*
by Leslie Davis Guccione

*Our Teacher Is Missing*
by Mary Francis Shura

# WHY ME?

## Deborah Kent

AN
**APPLE**
PAPERBACK

SCHOLASTIC INC.
New York  Toronto  London  Auckland  Sydney

12 11 10 9 8 7 6 5 4 3 2          3 4 5 6 7/9

Printed in the U.S.A.

First Scholastic printing, December 1992

# Acknowledgments

I wish to express my sincere thanks to Judith Stein, Nancy Majkowski, and their colleagues at Children's Memorial Hospital in Chicago. Their generous sharing of time and knowledge helped bring this book into being.

# 1

"*Jetés!*" Miss Panova cried. "One, two, three, four!"

The music shifted from the slow, gliding *adagio* rhythms to the bright, bouncing beat of our jumps and leaps. This final portion of class, the *allegro*, was my favorite. It came as a reward after the long, steady, warm-up exercises, which took up most of the hour. *Allegro* was our chance to let go of the ground, to fly.

Some days, I seemed to fit into the music as though it were made just for me. It swept me away, light as a snowflake, effortless as thought. Those were the times I lived for, the moments I earned with all of the hours of practice, the aching calf muscles, and sprained feet. But today I was all wrong. I moved in slow motion, lost somewhere half a beat behind everyone else. I thumped down hard on my heels, and my head throbbed each time my feet hit the floor. My body felt heavy and thick, like a lump of bread dough that wouldn't rise. I could still follow the steps, but I couldn't pretend that I was dancing.

At last Miss Panova punched the button on the cassette player, and the room plunged into a grim silence. Slowly, drearily, I came down flat-footed to the floor and let my hands dangle at my sides.

For long seconds Miss Panova gazed above our heads at the Bolshoi poster by the door. She was the kind of teacher you longed to please. When she was happy with me, I felt like turning somersaults. But when I didn't measure up to what she expected, I wanted to shrivel up and disappear.

My head swam, and I tried to focus on the little rectangles in the wooden floor of the studio. I was beyond hope this afternoon. I was coming down with something — something that threw my body off balance and blurred my mind. But from her advanced students, Miss Panova never had much patience with excuses. Unless you pulled a muscle or sprained an ankle, she expected you to be in class, giving it your best.

"Tina, you're looking very good," she began. "You've been working hard these last few weeks, and it shows."

Tina flushed with pleasure. It was true, she had been having trouble with her *grand plié* for a while, but now she had it just right.

Miss Panova turned to Lici. "Alicia, you were lagging. Maybe you hear your own song inside your head — but in class, you better listen to the same piece the rest of us can hear."

I threw Lici a sympathetic glance, but she didn't notice. She looked up at Miss Panova and nodded, taking her punishment bravely.

For just an instant I let myself believe that I hadn't been quite as bad as I thought. Maybe Miss Panova wasn't going to say anything about me after all. But I'd been studying ballet for five years now, ever since I was eight. I knew enough to be my own judge.

"Rachel Whitaker." I swayed with the impact as my name crashed over me. Seven heads twisted around to stare. "Rachel, I don't quite know where to begin. You're dead weight on your feet, your body's off center half the time. I noticed it on Monday, but I thought it would pass. It just isn't like you to slide like this. You're sleepwalking," she added with a thin smile. "Wake up and smell the coffee!"

As she went on through the list, critiquing each member of the class, I sagged beneath the weight of her disappointment. I should have skipped class today. I'd felt bad to start with, but now Miss Panova's criticism was giving me a stomachache, too.

Once class was behind us, we always went a little wild. But today not even the dressing-room banter perked me up. Tina got going with a Madonna routine in front of the mirror. Then Joy told a long, crazy story about her cousin Samantha, who was such a klutz she managed to break her leg playing Ping-Pong. Sarah went into stitches until she dropped a bottle of perfume, and the whole place smelled like lily of the valley.

Any other day, I would have been in the middle of the action. But I couldn't find the energy this afternoon. My head pounded harder with every passing minute. And there was something else. Something had been looming over me since this morning, but I couldn't think what it was.

I retreated to a bench in the corner and tugged off my leotard. My fingers felt stiff and sluggish as I folded it into its plastic bag. My hands looked oddly swollen, puffy at the wrists and the finger joints. When I looked down at my feet, I thought my ankles seemed to be swelling, too.

Just because I'd had some weird bug a couple of weeks ago, I didn't have to turn into a hypochondriac. It had been really spooky — like a stomach virus, only my joints ached, too, and I broke out all over in itchy purple blotches. Dr. Hill never did figure out what it was, but it went away by itself. I'd been fine for a while now.

Lici dropped onto the bench beside me and slipped on her shoes. "Not exactly our day, huh?"

I shrugged and pulled my sweater over my head. I didn't feel much like talking.

"I can't wait till Saturday," she said. "It's going to be so neat!"

"Yeah, right," I muttered. Saturday night our whole class was going to Orchestra Hall to see the Moscow Ballet. I'd been excited ever since Miss Panova told us about the tickets. But now I was too sodden and dragged out to care.

I felt clearer as soon as we got into the fresh air and started for the bus stop. But gazing out at the stores and the hurrying shoppers on the ride up Milwaukee Avenue, I knew that something horrible hung over me, just out of reach, waiting to hurtle down.

For some reason, the bus's bottom step seemed higher than usual, and I almost lost my footing as we got off. "You okay?" Lici asked, touching my shoulder.

"I'm fine!" I flared, jerking free. "Why shouldn't I be?" I hadn't expected to sound so angry. A pained look flicked across her face. I tried laughing at myself, to show her I was sorry. "I'm turning into a super klutz," I said. "Joy's cousin Samantha had to play Ping-Pong to break her leg. I can do it getting off the Milwaukee Avenue bus."

Lici lived about a block from the bus stop, so by tradition I hung out with her for a while after ballet. She was the only girl in my class at school who also studied with Miss Panova. Lici was one of the first people I met when we moved to Chicago last year and I had to face seventh grade in a brand-new school. It was wonderful to discover that Lici and I had *pliés* and *battements* in common. Outwardly, we couldn't have been much more different. But we both truly cared about ballet. It was something special we shared which few other people completely understood.

Lici's little sister, Ana, sat on the wide, wooden porch, sorting through her herd of Rainbow Ponies. She was a smaller version of Lici, dark and petite, with a thick black braid down her back.

"Hey, Ana! Stick out your tongue!" Lici cried, bounding up the steps.

Ana set a pink-spangled pony on the railing and stared. "Why?"

"You've got to," Lici told her. "It's in the interest of science. You've got to stick out your tongue and see if you can roll up the sides of it, like this." Lici's tongue popped out and rolled up to form a long pink trough.

"Ee-ew! Gross!" Ana cried. "What kind of science is that?"

"It's this project for school." Lici turned to me, waiting for me to confirm what she said. But I was starting to feel sick again. My stomach was rolling around as though I were out sailing in a hurricane. I managed a nod, but I let her do the talking.

"We've got to make this family tree, and show

who can roll their tongue and who can't," Lici went on. "It's to show about genes and heredity, all that stuff. I've got to test everybody. Aunt Matilda and Uncle Berto and all the cousins, even Grandma and Grandpa Flores. *That* ought to be a riot!"

Ana drew a circle in the air next to her temple. "You're cra-azy!" she drawled. "Can you just see Grandma Flores sticking her tongue out and making these faces?" Just to make her point, she stuck out her own tongue and rolled it as neatly as Lici did.

Pretty soon the whole clan was out on the porch — Lici's three big brothers, a couple of girl cousins who'd dropped over, Lici's mom, and her aunt Matilda with her new baby. They laughed and chattered in a patchwork of Spanish and English, trying to outdo each other making faces like those gargoyles you see on ancient stone churches.

I watched from the bottom step, at the fringe of the crowd. I could never be around Lici's family for long without a twinge of envy. They always had so much fun! They were all parts of a whole — playing together, belonging to each other.

After a while the baby began to fuss, and Aunt Matilda packed up her diaper bag to head home. Lici's mom went in to cook, and the brothers wandered out to the yard to pitch a baseball back and forth. A cousin or two trailed after them to cheer them on. "I better get going," I told Lici. "I've got a ton of homework."

"You going to start your tongue-rolling chart?" she asked. "It's not due till after Thanksgiving, don't forget. So you can test all your relatives when they come over for turkey dinner, right?"

"I'm not going to waste my time on that!" I said, kicking at the step. "If Mr. Ciardi thinks I'm going to pester everybody with that tongue stuff, he's nuts."

Lici sighed and shook her head. I was always protesting about something, and by now she didn't take my complaints very seriously. But I meant it this time.

"It won't be so hard," she assured me. "You saw how everybody got giggling and — "

"It's stupid! They've got no right to make me do it!"

Lici stepped back and looked at me as if she thought I'd gone around the bend. "What are you talking about?" she demanded. "It's just an assignment."

"I can't do that chart!" I knew I was getting a little too worked up. But somehow I felt as though that simple science project was responsible for my pounding head, my disastrous performance in class, for everything that was wrong about today. "All that about what you inherit from which side — I just can't! It's not fair!"

8

"Okay, cool it, will you!" Lici said. "What isn't fair? I don't get it."

I gripped my armload of books and drew a long, steadying breath. I was being ridiculous, I knew I was. I had to get myself under control.

After a couple of seconds, I thought I could speak without a quaver in my voice. "There's a reason why I can't do this project. I can't draw a nice little tree and show some pattern about my family heredity." I stopped for another breath, and flung out the words at last. "The reason is — I'm adopted."

# 2

"**H**ow come you never told me?"

That was a logical question. Lici was my best friend. I'd told her every tortured detail of my crush on Danny Kuczinski, right down to the last wink and giggle. She knew I kept a secret diary, that I couldn't stand spiders, that I always cried when I watched *E.T.* So why hadn't I told her I had been adopted? It was just an everyday ordinary fact of my life.

Now that I thought about it, I realized I hadn't mentioned that I was adopted to anyone here in Chicago. I had so many more urgent things to think about, trying to make new friends and learning to survive in a big city, that it never came up.

I guess my parents told me I was adopted as soon as I was old enough to talk. I remember that once, when I was three or four, the plumber came to fix the kitchen sink, and I ran to the door and greeted him, "I'm adopted! I'm special!" I didn't really understand what I was saying. I was just repeating words I'd heard a hundred times, the way our parakeet chanted, "Prettyboy, prettyboy!"

I think that from reading a lot of pamphlets, my parents got the idea they had to persuade me that having been adopted was a blessing. "You were chosen," Mom would say when I was little. "We wanted you, that makes you a very special person." But then in the next sentence she'd say that having been adopted didn't really matter, because we were just a regular family, and I was like everyone else.

Of course, when Mom had my sister, Phoebe, I found out that *not* having been adopted was pretty special, too. I suppose it comes as a shock to any five-year-old, the arrival of a squalling little creature that everybody adores, no matter how it disrupts the household. I was no longer the reigning princess. I had been deposed. I remember wondering sometimes, in those first few years, whether Mom and Dad loved Phoebe more than they loved me. I felt like she was really theirs, while I was some stranger's kid they had taken in.

Actually, though, Phoebe turned out to be a pretty neat kid, and little by little I got over my jealousy. By now I knew that she didn't rate any extra privileges. She got yelled at for spilling jelly on the carpet or cutting up Dad's *Newsweek*, the same way I did when I was eight. Most of the time she was so bound up in her own world that she wasn't even much of a pest.

But now and then — when the relatives flocked in at Christmas, or when we went to Cape Cod in the summer to spend a week with Grandma and Grandpa Whitaker — someone would cast Phoebe a long, hard look and ask, "Who do you think she takes after?" And it would hit me with a little jolt that, as long as I lived, nobody was ever going to ask that question about me.

After I outgrew the "I was adopted, I'm special" stage, the subject gradually faded from family discussions. But I couldn't help being curious. Once, when I was eleven, I asked Mom if she knew anything about my real parents. She got upset and said that she and Dad *were* my real parents, the parents who had loved me and cared for me since I was three days old. I guess I used the wrong words. I only ended up hurting her feelings, and I didn't get an answer to my question.

Another time, just last year, I saw a show on TV about a man who had been adopted and had tracked down the woman who was his birth mother. I had never imagined such a thing was possible, but this guy explained that there were people all over the country doing searches now, even changing laws to read old adoption records that used to be sealed up for secrecy.

I was perched on the edge of the couch, utterly engrossed, when Dad walked in. He listened for about fifteen seconds, just long enough to hear what the program was about, and then he switched the channel to some business report. I was stunned. He never acted like that if I was watching *General Hospital*, or doing my homework with MTV in the background. I opened my mouth to protest, but the look on his face stopped me. Without a word, he told me that he felt my watching that show, thinking those questions, was a kind of betrayal. I shouldn't wonder about the family I was born into. I was a Whitaker now.

But I didn't look like one. Mom and Dad were tall and slender, with thick, dark hair and faces that looked as though they generally saw the serious side of life. They say married people start to resemble each other after a while, and it was certainly true in their case. That was probably why Grandma Whitaker and Aunt Bea were always trying to figure out who Phoebe took after. Mom and Dad looked so much alike that it was anybody's guess.

I didn't look like any of them. I was five-foot-one and had red hair, and my freckles made me look like some mischievous kid in a comic strip who just got caught with her hand in the cookie jar. When we moved to Chicago last year, our new next-door neighbor, Mrs. Ulasovitch, thought I was the baby-sitter.

"Well, why?" Lici was asking again.

The temperature was dropping, too cold for

September. I buried my hands in the pockets of my jacket, but they still felt icy. "I guess it didn't seem that important," I said.

"How can you say it's not important, when you're getting all freaked out about this science assignment?"

"I'm not freaked out!"

"Well, you know what I mean. If it's not important, then — "

"It isn't like it's this big issue in my life," I tried to explain. "It's not some gigantic emotional problem."

"But you must wonder, don't you? About who you were really born to, and why they couldn't keep you?"

"Sure," I admitted. "But it's dumb. I'll never find out, probably, so it's a waste of time." I shrugged my shoulders, trying to get rid of the whole subject. "Maybe I'll just fake that family heredity thing. Draw Phoebe's instead of mine."

"Yeah, you could get away with that, I guess," Lici said. She looked thoughtful, her lower lip caught between her teeth. "If I were you, I'd wonder all the time who my real mother was," she said after a moment. "Do you ever make up stories about her?"

"My birth mother? Once in a while," I admitted. "I call it the Mother Game."

"What if she's somebody glamorous, like a movie star or a great dancer or something? Maybe some day she'll find you and take you to Hollywood."

"I'm not holding my breath," I said. "With my luck, she'd turn out to be Frankenstein's bride."

Lici and I said good-bye, and I headed home. My house was about two blocks beyond Lici's, over near the park. I was crossing the street when a wave of nausea made me clap my hand over my mouth. I staggered to the curb and sat down, breathing deeply, until it finally passed.

For years I had trained my body to obey me. I could turn my legs out from the hip, I could do a perfect split, and rise gracefully on my toes. But sometimes lately I wondered if my body was turning against me. I was helpless, in the clutches of an enemy I couldn't name.

Headlights rushed toward me, and a car swept past. I couldn't just sit there like that. Sooner or later, someone would stop and ask what was the matter.

Cautiously I stood up. The earth was solid under my feet. It was mind over matter, as Dad would say. I'd be fine if I refused to get sick again.

Maybe I'd been feeling peculiar because of that science assignment. It was all — what was that word? — all psychosomatic. Just in my head. Ridiculous, to get sick over a family tree.

"Rachel, is that you?" Mom called as I unlocked the front door.

"Hi, it's me," I said. I dropped my books on the

couch and tossed my jacket over the back of a chair.

Mom came in from the kitchen with a dishtowel draped over one arm. "We're going to eat a little early tonight," she said. "Your father has to see a client at seven-thirty."

The thought of food was repulsive. And in my family, everybody had to sit down together at the dinner table. No excuses were accepted.

Mom stepped closer. "Do you feel all right?" she asked. "You look a little pale."

For a moment I longed to tell her about the day I'd been having. No, it wasn't only today, I reminded myself. It had been coming on since last weekend — the headaches, the queasiness, and then that other weird problem I'd started to notice. Lately I didn't have to go to the bathroom very often. I just didn't have to pee.

I could just picture the fuss Mom would make if I told her all that. She'd drag me off to the doctor, and they'd poke and prod and who knew what they'd decide about me. If I just waited it out, I would get better by myself.

"Mother!" I exclaimed. "I'm fine!"

"You're sure?" she asked. "Maybe it's just the light in here."

She was heading for the floor lamp in the corner, when Phoebe bounced in with the distraction I needed. "This is the neatest puzzle!" she chattered. "You can put it together forty-eight different ways, and I found three already."

Crouching at the coffee table, she shook out a box of plastic pieces. "Look! You've got to get them all to fit back in. Try it, Rae."

I knew at one glance I wouldn't be able to put the thing together. But I jumped at the chance to get Mom's mind off the state of my health. I squatted down next to Phoebe and pushed the pieces into a pile. Some were square, some rectangular, some T-shaped or L-shaped, and one looked like the state of Utah. At first they all seemed willing to fit snugly into the box. But when I got down to the last three, I realized there was going to be one left over.

"Let me," Phoebe said. She slid the box toward her and dumped it out again. In two minutes she had all of the pieces in place. "That's Method Number One," she announced, grinning. "Forty-seven more to go."

Mom watched for a while, offering suggestions, and I could tell she was itching to try it herself. She was almost as fascinated by puzzles as Phoebe was. I made a bet with myself that by Phoebe's bedtime they'd be up to Method Number Fourteen.

I wondered if that kind of talent was inherited — the ability to work puzzles. It seemed to go hand in hand with a knack for understanding computers and solving math problems. Mom was a programmer, and Phoebe already knew at least two computer languages. Sometimes when I listened to them talking about bytes and rams, I felt like I came from another planet.

Once in a while Dad would watch Mom and Phoebe playing computer games, or getting excited over some mathematical brain-teaser, and shake his head. He said it all reminded him too much of work. He sold life insurance, and he spent a lot of time studying complicated charts called actuarial tables, trying to figure a client's likelihood of dying young. But he must have been good at math, too, or he wouldn't have picked a job like that in the first place.

Well, I consoled myself, they could outchase me in any numbers match, but they were all hopeless klutzes. When Phoebe tried to do ballet exercises with me, she usually wound up tripping over the rug, or bumping into a chair.

After a while Mom said she had to stir the vegetables, and disappeared into the kitchen again. I collected my books and started to go up to my room. But in the front hall I caught a glimpse of myself in the mirror, and stopped short. My hair was as tangled as a Halloween witch's, and my eyes stared from a pale, puffy face. No wonder Mom had asked me if I felt all right!

I hunted a comb out of my purse, and smoothed my hair back into shape. A few dabs of lipstick brought some life back to my face. But I still wasn't what you'd call the picture of health.

There was something absurd about standing in front of the mirror, patching myself up. I felt as if I were watching myself from outside, viewing a movie about some forlorn waif trying to prepare for an audience with the queen. The problem was that I looked too sad and mopey to fool anybody. Makeup wouldn't improve me for long, whatever the lighting.

I pushed my lips into a smile. There, that was a little better, but it didn't look as if I meant it. I pictured Tina flouncing through her Madonna imitation, and the smile grew bigger, more natural.

Then I started to get silly. I wrinkled my nose and blew up my cheeks for a clown mask. I stuck my tongue out at my grinning reflection, and it stuck its tongue out at me. Before I realized what I was about to do, I contorted my face and tried to roll the sides of my tongue up to form a trough.

I couldn't do it. I crossed my eyes and sucked in my cheeks and jutted out my chin, put my face through a whole parade of grimaces, but my tongue refused to obey orders.

"That makes four!" Phoebe called from the living room. "This one was really hard. Come here, Rae, you want to see?"

"Yeah," I told her, walking into the living room. "But first I want to ask you something."

"What?" she demanded.

"If you stick out your tongue, can you kind of

19

roll it up? Lift up the sides of it toward the mid-dle?"

"*What?*"

"You heard me right. I'm not kidding. Can you?"

"I don't know." She hesitated. "Promise you won't laugh at me?"

"Promise."

She opened her mouth, squeezed her eyes shut, stuck out her tongue, and rolled it like a pro.

# 3

The next morning, the world as I had always known it smashed to smithereens.

In the first moment after I awoke, I didn't notice that anything was wrong. Thin, pale sunlight crept between the curtains, and I realized it must still be very early. My alarm hadn't sounded yet, and the house was wrapped in stillness. I could burrow under the covers and go right back to sleep.

Then I tried to roll over.

My head had turned to stone. It was so heavy I could barely move it on the pillow. I tried to push myself up with my hands, but they were stiff and unwieldy, and they hurt when I pressed down. My legs were two immense tree limbs. Each time I tried to move, pain rocketed through my skull, forcing me to lie where I was. It was as though an evil magician had come deep in the night, and cloaked me in some ghoulish enchantment.

"Mom!" My mouth was dry, and my voice squeaked out wispy and fragile.

I wanted to run, wanted my legs to carry me far away from whatever this was. But I could barely toss back the covers. "Mom!" I called again. "Help me!"

No one would ever hear me. I would lie here for hours alone, crying, hurting. What would happen to me if I didn't get help soon? Was I going to die?

The thought cut through me like a jagged splinter of glass. I couldn't be dying! I'd been dancing just yesterday, and tomorrow was the Moscow Ballet at Orchestra Hall. Something awful was wrong, but it couldn't be bad enough to snatch me away from everything I knew and loved. No, I wasn't going to die, I was going to be fine as soon as my mother came in.

I forced myself upright, and teetered on the edge of the bed. My voice pierced the stillness of the early-morning house in one tremendous effort. *"MOM!"*

Light flooded in as my door clicked open. For an instant I imagined that I was three years old again, waking out of a nightmare about monsters and quicksand. My mother was here to make everything bright and safe.

"What's the matter?" she asked. "It's only six-thirty."

"I'm — sick." Thick fog spiraled down to engulf

22

me. I couldn't sit up any longer. I sagged backward, sprawling diagonally across the bed.

"Rachel!" Mom leaned above me, and a look of terror flashed across her face. Then she was gone.

I remember the pounding of footsteps on the stairs, the faraway ring of the telephone, and Dad's voice somewhere, sharp with decision.

Then Mom was back, handing me my bathrobe. I half heard her long explanation about how she couldn't reach Dr. Hill, because he didn't get in until ten. So his answering service said that if I was really sick they should take me to the emergency room.

To my surprise, I could walk. Down the stairs I went, with Mom on one side and Dad on the other. The next thing I knew, I was huddled on the backseat of the station wagon. "But I'm not even dressed!" I said. "I can't go out in my nightgown."

No one answered. Maybe I only wanted to say it, but didn't quite put together the words. The thought of what I was wearing turned around and around inside my head. I was wrapped up in something warm and soft that tickled under my chin. It must be Aunt Bea's afghan, with the fringe on the edge. But I couldn't arrive at the hospital bundled up in an afghan! It would come unwound when I tried to walk, and everybody would laugh.

I must have dozed, or fainted, because I don't remember anything else until a blast of cool air struck my face, and I opened my eyes to discover a sea of parked cars. Strange, brusque hands tucked the afghan around me, and I began to move, feet first, wheels rumbling me over the pavement. That thick, sluggish feeling weighed down my mind, and I couldn't make sense of anything.

"Mom?" I asked cautiously. "Dad?"

"We're right here," Mom said from somewhere behind my head. "You're going to be okay."

Of course I was going to be okay. I had to get up pretty soon, get dressed, go to school. Lici was going to meet me before the bell.

We were at the hospital. It was just how I'd pictured it, from those doctor shows on TV. Bright lights beamed into my face, and figures in white scurried in and out of my line of vision. From where I lay I could only glimpse fragments of the people who passed — a bald head in profile, an outstretched arm, a pair of lumbering shoulders, a disappearing back. A loudspeaker shouted, "Doctor Orsolini! Doctor Orsolini! Please call two-six-three-four!"

"Can you hear me?" a dark-haired nurse asked.

"It's not my ears!" I said impatiently. "I just feel — awful!"

The nurse slid an icy cold stethoscope down inside the neck of my nightgown. I tried to flinch away, but my head thudded whenever I moved.

"Try to sit up," she said. "I have to listen to you breathe."

As she slipped her hand under my back and helped me up, the afghan slithered down around my waist, and there I was, for all to see, in my flowered robe. ". . . knew that would happen," I panted. I would have laughed, except that breathing took so much of my energy.

"Have you been passing urine regularly?" the nurse asked.

Wasn't it already embarrassing enough, sitting here half-dressed, without some stranger asking me how often I peed? "I don't know," I muttered. I wished she would let me lie down again.

"Try to think," the nurse insisted. "Did you go this morning? Do you have to go now?"

"No," I said. "No, not really."

The nurse nodded to herself, as though I had just proved some theory. "We're going to draw some blood," she explained. "Then we're going to admit you. Your mother's filling out the forms."

I closed my eyes. Voices rattled around me. A siren wailed. Somewhere a child was crying — low, weary sobs that went on and on. They were going to admit me. That meant sign me in, make me stay here no matter how much I wanted to leave. Not that I was capable of going anywhere, the way I felt.

Even then, muddled as my thinking was, I re-

alized that I was sick — very sick — and I was
going to stay sick for a long time.

There is nothing in the world more undignified
than being in the hospital. They had tubes and
needles sticking into me everywhere. I was in one
of those big high beds with metal rails on the sides,
sort of like a baby's crib, and every few minutes
some resident would come in to ask me questions,
or a nurse would want to take my temperature or
draw another blood sample.

Late in the morning a woman came in and introduced herself as Dr. Wong. Mom and Dad
trailed after her, their faces somber.

"Rachel, we've done some tests about the function of your kidneys," Dr. Wong explained. "The
blood tests show it's down. Down very low."

What was she talking about? All those blood
tests . . . What did blood have to do with kidneys?
Very low . . . I could tell by the way she said it —
very low meant bad.

Dr. Wong was still talking. "This is a serious
condition. We must take steps right away."

Suddenly I was fully alert. "What do you mean,
a serious condition?" I demanded. "What steps?
What's wrong with me, anyway?"

"You have Henoch Schonlein purpura," Dr.
Wong said, as though that would explain everything. "The name is hard, we just say HSP. This
causes the kidneys to fail."

26

"Henoch what?"

"I'll spell the name," Dr. Wong suggested. "H-e-n-o-c-h S-c-h-o . . ." My mind drifted away from the tide of letters. None of it meant anything good.

Mom and Dad drew closer to the bed. They tilted together as though they were trying to hold one another up. "It's part of that problem you had before," Dad said. "With the rash and — "

·"But I'm over that!" I cried. "That was weeks ago!"

"It can be very difficult to diagnose at first," Dr. Wong was saying. "It's an infection, related to strep. The bacteria remain in your system."

Mom tried to pick up where Dad left off. "Doctor Wong explained it to us in her office. Your kidneys have stopped working. That's what's making you feel sick."

I listened in a daze as Dr. Wong talked on, about chemical impurities that build up in the blood. Her long tangled words floated past me and were gone. But at last I heard something that sounded important, and I tried to hang onto what she was saying. If the kidneys were not working to filter these chemicals out of the bloodstream, then it was necessary to use artificial methods.

Everyone was quiet. Out in the corridor dinner trays clattered, and women's voices rose in laughter. "What's going to happen to me?" I asked. My voice was shaking. "What are you going to do?"

For long seconds no one answered. In the silence I sensed that each of them — Mom, Dad, and even Dr. Wong — was hoping that someone else would explain.

"Come on!" I cried. "Somebody tell me!"

Dad's voice was muffled, as though he were speaking through layers of fabric. "They're going to start you on special treatments. It's called dialysis."

# 4

It all happened too fast, that was the trouble. Maybe if I'd had some warning, if I'd had a couple of weeks to get used to the idea, it would have been easier. But probably nothing could have prepared me for the reality of dialysis.

The first time, that Thursday I went into the hospital, they swabbed my stomach with something to numb the skin. I was lying on a padded table, looking up at the lights on the ceiling, when I glimpsed a needle about the size of my arm. "My name is Elena," the nurse said. "This really won't hurt much, I promise you. We're just going to put some fluid into your abdomen. It's a special solution that helps to cleanse your blood. It'll sit there for a couple of hours, and as the blood passes through it the fluid draws out the toxic chemicals that are normally filtered by your kidneys."

I wasn't interested in a scientific explanation. I just wanted to survive that needle.

The needle was attached to a coil of plastic tubing, and at the other end of the tube was a heavy plastic bag full of clear liquid. Shivering with terror, I watched the nurse hang the bag on a rack above me. I squeezed my eyes shut as she took the needle from her instrument tray.

At least she had told me the truth. I felt the pressure when she stuck me, but it really didn't hurt much. I opened my eyes in time to see her taping the needle into place.

"Comfortable?" she asked brightly.

"Oh, sure," I said. "Never felt better."

"It takes a little getting used to," she admitted. "But after a few times it gets as routine as brushing your teeth."

She reached up and opened a plastic clamp on the tubing below the bag. I watched with macabre fascination as the liquid snaked down the tube toward me.

"What do you mean, after a few times?" I demanded. "I'm not doing this again, believe me."

"I wish it worked that way," she said, sighing. She opened another clamp, this one just above the place where the needle went in. I didn't feel anything much at first, but little by little my stomach began to seem full. It was as if I'd just drunk a gallon of water and it was all sloshing around down there. Pretty soon the plastic bag hung flat and empty. Elena disconnected the tubes and pulled out the needle.

"In a couple of hours we'll drain the solution out

and put some more in," she explained. She dabbed my stomach with some sort of antiseptic, and stuck a bandage over the spot where the needle had been.

I sat up shakily. I looked around, dazed, trying to grasp what had happened to me. I was wide awake. The mattress, the white walls, Elena's hands helping me down from the table were all real. But none of it made sense.

"You may not feel much better with this first treatment," Elena warned me. "It's going to take a while to get your levels into the normal range. But by tomorrow you'll be up and around."

"I feel all blown up," I said. "Like a water balloon."

"I know," Elena said. "All my patients say it feels funny at first. But after a few days you won't notice it anymore."

There it was again — that sidelong reference to dialysis in my future. I didn't want to hear about it. But I had to know.

The room wobbled as I stood up. Elena eased me into a wheelchair. "How long am I going to be on this dialysis business anyway?" I asked. "When will I be better?"

Elena leaned against the edge of the table. She looked down at me, frowning. "Didn't your doctor explain it to you?" she asked.

I shook my head. "I guess she tried to," I said. "But I was too bummed out to listen real well."

"Your kidneys have failed," Elena told me bluntly. "They've been destroyed by the disease you had — HSP. The kidneys are vital organs, right?"

I nodded to prove I was following and she went on. "If your kidneys don't work you can't live. Dialysis is an artificial way of doing the work of the kidneys. Okay — you know your kidneys, when they're working properly, they're on duty all the time. Twenty-four hours a day, cleaning up your blood so you feel good and healthy."

She paused. "Mm-hmm," I prodded. When would she get to the point?

"Dialysis tries to do the job of the kidneys," Elena continued. "You can't just dialyze once and" — she snapped her fingers — "and you're all set for the rest of your life. It's not like that. It has to be on a regular schedule. It has to be part of your everyday life."

"I can't spend the rest of my life in this place!" I cried. "It's not fair!"

"You don't have to stay here," Elena began. "You can come in three times a week for hemodialysis. With that you have a line attached to your wrist and your blood circulates through a machine to do the work of the kidneys. Or you can learn to dialyze at home — "

"Why did this have to happen to me?" I burst out. "I'm not going to live like that! I'd rather just die and get it over with!"

"I know it's a shock," Elena said. Her voice was soft, like a caress. "But, believe me, you'll get past this stage of it. You'll feel better and you'll adjust."

"I won't," I said sullenly. "I can't."

"Give it time," Elena said. "Go back up to your room and I'll see you tomorrow. Someone from the night shift will be by later to drain the solution and put some more in."

It sounded so disgusting. Draining out, filling up! That was *my body* she was talking about! *Me!*

I didn't answer. I sat hunched over my bloated belly, staring into space. After a while an aide came and wheeled me back up to my room.

"Hey, where did they take you?" chirped a voice from the bed by the window. "Did you go down to PT?"

A girl of about ten peered at me through the rails. She had big dark eyes and a spiky Afro. I didn't remember seeing her this morning, but she may have been there all the time and I'd just been too sick to notice. One of her legs was encased in a heavy plaster cast.

"Did you?" she repeated. "Did you go to PT or what?"

"I don't even know what PT is," I said. The nurse's aide helped me out of the wheelchair and back into bed. I thanked her and sank against the pillows.

"PT, that's therapy," my roommate explained

33

patiently, as though it were one of those basics everybody was supposed to know. "It's like where you go to exercise your leg or your arms. Man, I go to PT twice a day!"

"I went to dialysis." At least I'd better get used to saying the word. Dialysis was going to be with me for a long, long time.

My roommate's name was Zila Mae. She said she lived in a housing project called the Taylor Homes, with her grandmother and two aunts and more cousins than I could keep track of. She chattered all evening, telling me the plots of her favorite TV shows, recounting her dreams, and filling me in on her adventures in her neighborhood. Pretty soon I didn't know which stories were real and which were fiction. I wished I could flip a switch and turn her off.

"Hey," I finally interrupted her, "you know how to play Rock, Scissors, Paper?"

She didn't, but she caught on in an instant. It was fun, for about three minutes. But Zila Mae wasn't about to quit. After half an hour I hid my hands under the covers and told her I was going to sleep. She was sleepy, too, I could tell. Her voice grew slower and slower. She left long pauses between sentences. And at last she faded completely.

For the first time in this strange, terrible day, I was alone. No one stood by to defend me from my thoughts, and they swarmed in for the attack. My kidneys had failed me. For thirteen years they had behaved without a hitch, and I had never appreciated them, never given them any credit. Now they had betrayed me. I dangled over a bottomless pit. Death. I was so close to it I could invite it to take me. All I had to do was refuse dialysis. Only dialysis could keep me alive.

I slid into a ragged sleep. But each time I woke, cold terror seized me again. I had almost died. The unthinkable, the impossible was happening to me.

Sometime during the night another nurse came in with her needle and her tubes and bags. She stuck me again and slowly my swollen stomach went flat. I glanced over just once, and saw a bag filling with yellowish liquid. After about twenty minutes, she disconnected it and clamped on one of those overhead bags to fill me up again. She tried to show me how the equipment worked, but I closed my eyes and wouldn't talk. Maybe if I ignored it hard enough, dialysis would go away.

Morning arrived with the clatter of breakfast trays and another thermometer, another pill. Then Elena came in with a big smile, ready for another cheerful exchange of fluids and bags. And when I sat up, I really did feel better. Perhaps the treatment actually worked.

"How can you stand doing this every day?" I asked. "Pouring gallons of fluid in and out of people? Wouldn't you rather sell shoes or something?"

"Not gallons — it's about two liters," Elena said, as though it really made a difference.

"It's gross, whatever it is," I told her. "I don't want to look at it."

I braced myself for another spiel on how I'd get used to all of this, but Elena was busy unclamping the next bag.

"Over the next few days we can talk about your choices for treatment," she said. "Some people prefer to come into the hospital and go on the hemodialysis machine. Others opt for CAPD. That's what we're giving you right now. You can learn to handle it all yourself and just come in for checkups every couple of weeks."

It was bad enough having a nurse stick me with needles and organize all those bags. I couldn't imagine doing it on my own. "What does CAPD stand for?" I asked. "Captured Alive, Pinned Down?"

"Ha-ha," Elena said. "It's continuous ambulatory peritoneal dialysis. Try repeating that one ten times."

I giggled. Elena was pretty nice. It helped — a little.

"You'd think medical science could come up with something better," I said. I tried to laugh again but it wasn't really that funny.

Elena hesitated. "There is another possibility," she said. "We'll talk about it when your parents come in. We could put your name on the list for a kidney transplant."

"An operation? Like they'd give me somebody else's kidney?"

"Right. You'd have to be on medication, and have some restrictions in your diet. But other than that you're pretty much back to normal if the transplant is successful."

"Really?" It was as though she had flung open a window, filling the room with fresh air. There *was* a way out. I'd known all along I couldn't be condemned to dialysis forever. An operation wouldn't be much fun, but once that part was over, I could walk away as though none of this had ever happened.

But of course there were gruesome details. "Sometimes," Elena said, "they use a cadaver kidney — "

"Eew! You mean out of a dead person?"

"It's still a living organ," Elena insisted. "Or there's the possibility of a live donor transplant. If you have someone who can donate for you, that's probably the best bet."

There were no nice neat solutions. Why had my body done this to me in the first place? Why did I have to think about all of this — and live with it, and go on living with it . . .

"Can just anybody donate a kidney?" I asked. "You know, like 'Here, I've got a spare, you want it?' "

"Well, no, it can't be just anybody," Elena said. "It has to be what we call a good genetic match, or your body will reject it. Usually a live donor is a parent or a sister or brother. It needs to be a close blood relative."

The window slammed shut. The room was stifling again. "Oh," I said. "That's all I need to know. I guess I'll be staying on dialysis after all."

I was in no mood to see anyone, but people paraded through my room all day long. About ten minutes after Elena left, Mom showed up with an armload of paperbacks, a box of colored pencils, and a huge pad of drawing paper to keep me entertained. If she hadn't come, I would have felt miserable and abandoned. But somehow having her there, with her long silences and determined little bursts of questions, felt like an invasion. She fluttered around, adjusting the TV, shifting my tray table, and making forays out to the nursing station to double-check my special diet.

"Just sit down," I told her finally. "Relax, okay?"

"Hospitals aren't made to relax in," Mom said, trying for a laugh. "One whiff of that smell in the hall, and tension sets in."

I knew what she meant. That blend of disinfectant, medicine, and stale meals was all tied up with my worst fears.

Mom had to be back at work by one, but as soon

as she left Elena came in for my next treatment. She gave me a pep talk about the joys of self-care — which meant learning to handle the bags and tubes myself.

"I can't do it," I told her flatly. "Don't even talk about it. I'll just let them put me on that machine. Then I can lie back and make believe it isn't happening."

"Well, that's one of your options," Elena said, in that tolerant voice people use to let you know they disapprove. "The thing is, though, you only come in three days a week, and between treatments there's time for a lot of stuff to build up in your system. You might feel dragged out a lot, get headaches, that sort of thing. If you're on CAPD, the treatment is continuous. Most patients feel quite a bit better."

I couldn't argue. She was trying to help me. I let her give me my first lesson, opening and shutting plastic clamps.

"It isn't so hard, once you get the hang of it," she said. "And we'll teach your parents, too, so they can help you at home."

I might as well forget ever having any privacy, ever again. From now on, other people would always be baring my belly, poking and prying, while I lay passive and helpless.

"I don't want people helping me," I declared. "If I have to do this, I'll do it myself."

Dad arrived just as Elena was packing up. He

brought a Minnie Mouse sticker book for Zila Mae, a transistor radio with headphones for me, and *The Wall Street Journal* for himself. At least I didn't have to invent a conversation as he thumbed through the Dow Jones reports. I switched on my favorite FM station, and for a little while the music pushed the world aside.

Then, as soon as she got off work, Mom was back, this time with Phoebe in tow. Phoebe had never been in a hospital before. "So many sick people all in one place!" she exclaimed. "Just coming up here I saw three people in wheelchairs, and a man with a neck brace, and a lady on a stretcher. It's awesome!"

In all my life I had never pictured myself in a place like this, surrounded by people who were all so ill. Not just surrounded by them — I was one of them. I wasn't an outsider like Mom and Dad and Phoebe. This was where I belonged.

At last they all left — Phoebe was starving. I was just lying back on the pillows, grateful for the quiet, when a nurse announced, "Rachel, you have another visitor." Peering shyly around the edge of the door was Lici.

She stepped into my hospital room straight from another world. "Miss Panova asked where you were," she chattered. "She asked the name of the hospital and everything — I bet she's going to send you a get-well card. And hey, guess what we found out?"

She paused expectantly, so I asked her, "What?"

"She's married! Honest! Her husband picked her up after class this afternoon. I mean, some of us were hanging out afterward, and she introduced him to us and everything! And you won't believe what he looks like!"

Again she paused, waiting for me to be excited. "What?" I said again.

"He's short, and he's got glasses, and he's bald on top — he looks like a professor or something. I mean, I just don't get it. She's so — chic. You'd think she'd be with somebody exciting, wouldn't you?"

"I don't know," I said. "I guess so."

"What's the matter?" Lici demanded. "You act like you aren't even listening!"

"What's the matter? I practically died yesterday, and I'm going to be on medications and these disgusting treatments for the rest of my life, and you're asking me what's the matter?"

Lici scraped back her chair, putting a little more distance between us. "I thought you'd want to hear what's going on. I thought it'd help, if I could take your mind off what's happening."

"You can't understand what it's like," I rushed on. "Nobody can. I'm trapped in this. There isn't a way out. My whole life is ruined!"

"It can't be," Lici insisted. "You'll get better. My aunt's a nurse, and she says this is the best hospital for kidney trouble. They'll get you fixed up."

"It isn't like that. What I've got is forever."

Lici groped for an answer. I ought to thank her for coming, I thought. I ought to tell her how glad I was that she'd taken the time to come out here on the bus just for me. But I didn't say a word. I just sat there and let her struggle.

At last she seemed to pull her thoughts together. "Even if you have to live with it, it won't be the only thing. Like, there'll still be ballet, and all the other kids, and — and everything that there always was."

"I know," I said. "Only it doesn't feel that way. I feel like I'll never be able to think about anything else besides my kidneys for the rest of my life."

# 5

Every day I did feel a little bit better. My head cleared, and my appetite came back with a vengeance. I thought about food all the time. The trouble was, there was hardly anything I was allowed to eat.

On my fourth day in the hospital, a dietician came in and explained that, on dialysis, I had to avoid potassium and sodium. "Sounds easy enough," I said. "I was never crazy about them anyway."

"Glad to hear it," she said with a forced little chuckle. "You should stay away from bananas, and potatoes, and anything that has a lot of salt, like chips or pretzels. Watch your protein. And of course keep your fluid intake down. Since you don't urinate on dialysis, you can't get rid of extra water."

"What if I'm thirsty?" I protested.

"You can have about a quart of fluid a day," the dietician said. "That includes foods that have liquid in them, like soups and Jell-O."

"Oh." I was beginning to get the picture. "What else?"

"Lay off the fruits and vegetables. Watch out for meat and cheese. Nuts are a definite no-no."

"Everything that's supposed to be good for you," I remarked.

"Keep away from chocolate," she continued. "Sweets in general aren't the greatest."

"Okay, okay. What *can* I eat?" I demanded.

She paused, trying to come up with something. "Well," she said at last, "you can have all the starches you want. Rice. And plenty of pasta — as long as there's no tomato sauce."

I fell asleep thinking of ice cream sundaes. I woke up longing for the taste of bacon and eggs. At lunchtime Zila Mae got a hamburger and French fries, and they brought me a sliver of chicken and a mound of rice.

But even worse than the hunger was the boredom. I think I would have lost my mind without my drawing paper and colored pencils. I had always loved to draw, and now I spent hours propped up in bed, sketching people and dogs and cats and vases of flowers. Zila Mae would bounce with glee every time I showed her a new picture. It was kind of nice to have such an appreciative audience.

Sometimes I filled up the empty hours by picturing our house. In my imagination I climbed the steps to the front porch, threw open the door, and stood in the narrow hallway. I saw the little round table where we dropped the mail, and Phoebe's roller skates kicked off in the corner. I transported myself into the living room, with the red velvet sofa, the rows of books along the wall, Dad's roll-top desk with its goosenecked lamp, and the aquarium bubbling contentedly under the window. It all seemed brighter and warmer than I had ever noticed before I got sick.

Then I would float up the stairs to my room on the second floor. Ballet pictures paraded across my bureau, and at the foot of my bed was the wooden rail that Dad had fastened to the wall to serve as my barre for practice. My good-luck pea-cock feather curled above the mirror. I had never realized what paradise it was, to have a room all to myself. I longed for it now, that oasis of quiet where no loudspeakers blared and no one in a uniform burst in to stab me with a needle. When I got home, I would cherish every moment of every day.

I could tell Dr. Wong had good news when she came in smiling one afternoon, during my second week on dialysis. "Rachel," she said, "how would you like to go home tomorrow?"

"Tomorrow?" I repeated. "You mean it?"

"I mean it," she said. "You are doing very well.

The nurses tell me you have learned self-care, so you can manage on CAPD. You are ready to leave us."

The news gave me a rush of energy. In five minutes I had all my things packed. I phoned Mom and Dad to tell them when they could pick me up. I called Lici and shouted in her ear that I was about to be liberated. Then I held the back of a chair and went through some barre exercises.

I was horribly out of shape from lying around for so long. But I could deal with that. My belly was another matter. I had a pretty good idea how it must feel to be pregnant — not huge, but more in that state that women call "starting to show." I showed all right — and that wasn't the worst part. The worst part of all was the tube.

On my third day of dialysis, just as I was starting to feel better, I had what Dr. Wong and Elena called "a minor surgical procedure." It may have seemed minor to them. They weren't the ones who had to have a plastic tube inserted in their abdomen, with about eight inches of it sticking out just below the belly button. It was all in the interest of making CAPD easier and more comfortable. No more needles. All I had to do was attach the protruding tube to the tube on a fresh bag of solution, unclamp, and *voilà!*

I had to admit that I didn't miss the needles. But if I wore anything tight, like a leotard, the tube would bulge. Even if I dressed so that no one else could see it, I would always know it was there.

After lunch the next day I put on my street clothes and played my last fifty-seven rounds of Rock, Scissors, Paper with Zila Mae. I was going to miss her. She became very quiet when I gave her my box of colored pencils as a good-bye present. "Man," she said after a remarkably long silence, "I wish you could stay here as long as me."

Mom took the afternoon off from work and arrived at two-fifteen, right on time. Behind her was an orderly, pushing an empty wheelchair. "Hop aboard!" he said, grinning.

"I can walk," I protested. "I've been up and walking all week!"

"Hospital regulation," he said. "We get you better, then we wheel you out. You make sense of it — I can't."

I couldn't either, but I didn't argue. I would have been glad to ride in a baby's stroller — anything that would carry me down the elevator, through the swinging doors, out into fresh air and motion and real life once more.

From the outside, our house looked comfortably familiar, as though I'd never been away. I ran up the steps and flung open the front door, just as I had done so many times in my imagination. But the living room looked shabbier than I expected. The drapes were drawn, and when I opened them to let in the sunlight, I discovered a film of dust on the furniture. Magazines had piled up on the coffee table, and in one corner lay a heap of newspapers that no one had carried out to the trash. In the kitchen, dirty dishes were stacked in the sink, and someone had left an empty pizza box on the counter.

The whole place had an air of discouragement and decay. I knew what was wrong. Mom and Dad had been so busy running back and forth to the hospital that they'd given up the fight against disorder. My kidney failure had disrupted their lives, too.

My room had a musty, closed-up smell, but it looked just as I had left it — until I opened the closet. Neatly arranged on the floor, where there used to be a jumble of shoes and broken hangers, stood two sturdy cartons marked MEDICAL SUPPLIES. One was filled with fat bags of dialysis solution, each trailing a coil of disposable tubing. The other contained the flat, folded bags for draining. I wasn't back to normal. Nothing would ever be normal again.

I sank onto the bed and buried my face in my hands. Suddenly, unbelievably, I wished I was back in the hospital again, with Elena and the other nurses standing by to help whenever I needed them. They'd taken me through the whole dialysis process step by step so many times, always encouraging me to do more and more myself.

By this morning I was an expert on "self-care." But now everything had rushed out of my head. I couldn't manage here, on my own. They were asking the impossible.

Well, I wasn't completely adrift. They had taught Mom and Dad how to help me. And they had reminded us there was always somebody on call at the hospital if we had a question.

Slowly they seeped back, all the unwelcome rules and procedures. I required four "exchanges" a day — one first thing in the morning, one at noon, one at five-thirty, and the last at bedtime. When I changed bags, everything must be sterile, sterile, sterile! No swimming, they warned. No tub baths, only showers. Infection was a very real danger. I couldn't be too careful.

Elena said I was a good patient. I was adjusting beautifully. She didn't hear the thoughts that tumbled around in my head. Actually, I only wanted to learn what they called "self-care" to assure myself some privacy. If I had to be on dialysis, I would do whatever I could to stay in charge.

Privacy had always been crucial at our house. Phoebe and I each had our own room, and even Mom and Dad had separate offices in the basement where they could work alone. I had learned to respect a closed door. It was an unspoken rule that you didn't intrude on others, and they didn't barge in on you.

I had stacks of makeup work to do for school. I

needed to turn on the music and work on my ballet exercises. I wanted to see Lici, to find out all the things that had happened while I was gone. If I could just gather my strength, I would get up and tackle the things that had to be done. But right now, I only wanted to rest. Just for a minute . . .

The slam of the front door jolted me awake. In the old days, before I got sick, I couldn't conceive of taking an afternoon nap. Now it seemed I couldn't function without one. Dr. Wong said I could go back to school Monday, and even return to ballet class. But how was I going to dance? They'd have to set up a cot for me in the dressing room so I could stretch out between routines.

Why had this happened to me, I asked myself for the hundredth time. I was an ordinary kid, not very different from anybody else. But this illness had pounced on *me* alone. I hadn't done anything to deserve it. I knew other people who were a lot worse than I was — people who cheated on tests, and lifted sweaters and earrings out of stores. Their bodies never turned against them. They went on without a twinge of pain.

Maybe I wouldn't have ended up on dialysis if I had told Mom when I first didn't feel well. But Dr. Wong said that by then the damage was done. It all went back to Dr. Hill, who hadn't realized my rash and joint pains were HSP. But even if he had known, even if he had prescribed the proper medications, I still might have developed kidney failure. It just happened, they said. Nobody knew why. It was just one of those events that struck at random, and there was nothing anyone could do.

Suddenly I wanted to smash something. I snatched up the first thing within reach and hurled it across the room. It struck the wall and shattered in a shower of tiny pieces.

Only then did I realize it was my favorite little ceramic keepsake box, the one with the butterfly on the lid. Lici had given it to me for my birthday. Now I had broken it. It was gone forever.

There was a knock at my door. "Rachel? Everything okay?" Mom called softly.

Hastily I swept the fragments into the corner. There was another unspoken rule in my family, besides the one about privacy. No matter what happened, you didn't make scenes. "I'm all right," I said. "Come on in."

"Phoebe's home," Mom said, pushing the door open. "She wants to see you, but I thought I better check first. See if you were awake."

"No telling, when you're dealing with me," I muttered.

She looked at me harder than I liked. "Dialysis is tiring," she said. "Doctor Wong explained that, remember? You'll just have to work your schedule around rest periods when you need them."

"Sure," I said. "Good days and bad days. I heard all that stuff."

"It's tough at first. You're still getting used to the treatments." Mom's voice was firm, but she twisted her hands together and gazed out the window as she talked.

"I don't want to get used to them!" I burst out. "I hate them! I don't want to spend the rest of my life blown up like a blimp! I might as well be — " I stopped short, just in time. I didn't really mean what I was about to say. I didn't want to die. I wanted to live.

"It might not be for the rest of your life," Mom said quietly. "Your name is on the list for a transplant. If they can find a donor — "

*"If,"* I repeated. I wouldn't let myself hope. Dr. Wong had explained that the waiting list for a cadaver donor was very long. Of course, if some relative offered to donate a kidney to me, that would be different.

It was just one more nasty trick of a nasty, teasing fate. I could wait till my hair turned gray, but no close relative would ever step out of the shadows to rescue me.

"Mom?" Phoebe's voice soared up to us. "Is she awake? Can I come up?"

"I'm coming," I hollered back. I couldn't let Phoebe know how down I felt. She was too little to understand. For her sake, I'd act calm and contented. I'd stick to the rule about not making scenes.

"Hi," she said almost shyly as I came

downstairs. "How do you feel, Rae?"

"I feel pretty good," I said. And I did, for the moment. That catnap had revived me a bit.

Phoebe studied me uneasily, as if she couldn't remember how to talk to me. I was home, but I didn't quite fit into the house the way I used to.

"I told Jerry — he's this boy in my class — I told him you're on dialysis," Phoebe said. "His mom says that they have to pump your blood through some kind of machine."

"Some people do that," I said. "I don't have to. It's just — oh, it's this special liquid to clean the bad stuff out of your blood."

"Can I see how it works?"

"I guess so. Maybe sometime." Perhaps I could put up a sign, charge admission to all the kids on the block.

"I get it!" Phoebe said, her face brightening. "It's kind of like toxic waste disposal. You know, like you see on the news, how they clean up the pollutants from the soil and the groundwater, right?"

"Yeah. Right." Phoebe sure had a knack for describing things! That was me, I thought grimly. My body was a living toxic waste dump. Four times a day the disposal unit tried to clean things up, but it didn't help for long. And unless my name came up on the transplant list, I was doomed to repeat the cycle week after week, year after year, without any end in sight.

# 6

"**A**nd Rachel, you're doing very nicely. You're getting right back into form."

Miss Panova didn't sound like herself. Her words were too soft, gummy, coated with syrup. They didn't protect me from what she really meant. We both knew that I was only getting by. My old zest was gone. I forced myself through practiced movements, but the heaviness in my belly dragged me down. I wore a long, loose blouse over my leotard to hide the ridge of the plastic tube. Lici said it was silly to conceal it; it just looked like a wrinkle. But that was Lici. She accepted things that other people thought were bizarre.

Sometimes, like today, an immense weariness rode on my back and I couldn't shake it off. *Ponderous*, that was the word that rose into my mind. I set one foot down, then the other — slowly, carefully, with all the grace and lightness of a buffalo.

For the past month, ever since I came back to class, Miss Panova had treated me as though I were in a special category. Instead of urging me toward excellence, she aimed me toward "good enough, under the circumstances."

Now she dismissed me with a stiff little nod that was meant to look like approval, and turned her attention to Lici. Lici needed work on her *glissades*, those quick, smooth little glides. Miss Panova called her out to the center of the floor, and took her through the movement again, honing every bend of the leg. They worked through it half a dozen times before she was satisfied.

I remembered the time back in the first week of school, when our phys ed teacher, Ms. Lundy, came out with the statement that, "True health is to live day to day without ever thinking about your body." Lici and I couldn't get over that one. For days afterward, I'd ask, "Have you given your body a thought lately?" and the two of us would double up laughing. But now I understood what Ms. Lundy had been talking about. I was aware of my body all the time. It was like a temperamental old car. Sometimes it didn't want to get started in the morning, and I had to prod and cajole it into action. Now and then it stalled out when I least expected trouble. And it needed constant tending if I were to keep it going at all.

I ate lunch in the nurse's office, while my dialysis bags filled and drained. Mrs. Walters, the nurse, let me sit in a little cubbyhole off her main office, where there was less chance that anyone would see me. Once Katie Rosario, one of the seventh-graders, wandered in with a skinned-up knee, and walked straight into my private den before Mrs. Walters spotted her. Katie stood and stared, as if her legs were frozen, and I wished I could die, right there on the spot, and never have to come face to face with another human being. I can't imagine what Katie thought. She mumbled, "Oh — I'm sorry," and fled, as though what I had might be catching.

Even sitting through classes I felt separate from the life around me. I was always distracted by some twinge or pain, worrying over the stomachache I'd had forty-five minutes ago, wondering how I would feel by the end of the day — thinking about my body.

I tried not to talk about it to anybody, not even to Lici. If I let myself get started, I'd sound like Grandma Whitaker on a bad arthritis day. I didn't have much to contribute to the average conversation, but I resolved not to be actively boring.

Perhaps I could drop my standard of wellness, learn to live a little more quietly and stoically than I had before I got sick. But I could never accept "good enough, under the circumstances" in ballet. Never.

I was pulling my pants on over my leotard, so no one would see me undressed, when Tina called,

"Hurry up, Rachel! He's out there right now! You can get a peek at him!"

"Who is?" I asked.

"Miss Panova's husband. You won't believe it. He looks like a gnome."

I slipped into my shoes and draped my coat over my arm. "Where is he?" I asked.

Lici pointed through the door. The others clustered behind me as I peered out. Sure enough, standing uncertainly with his back to the wall and his hands in his pockets, I saw a stubby little man with a mustache, glasses, and a shining bald head.

Instantly, overwhelmingly, I felt sorry for him. He looked so out of place, as though he knew he didn't belong here and wished he could vanish.

Tina tugged at my arm. "Isn't it grotesque?" she whispered. "How could Miss Panova pick somebody like that?"

I pulled away from her and put my coat on. "Oh, I don't know," I said impatiently. "What difference does it make?"

I glanced back once as I walked away, and saw them all staring after me. I should have tried to explain, but I couldn't, not without starting to cry. The trouble was that I knew how he felt, knew from the inside. When I looked at him, I saw a distorted reflection of myself — clumsy, misplaced, ridiculous. Miss Panova's studio was a shrine to grace and elegance. I was an impostor, pretending that I could still dance, that this heavy new version of myself could still be a pleasure to view. I was an insult to everything I had ever learned about ballet. I didn't deserve to be here any longer.

Mom was waiting out in the car to drive me to my four-thirty appointment at the hospital. "How was your day?" she asked. "Everything okay?"

I sat beside her, solidly belted in, but I felt as though I were losing my balance. I was tumbling down a murky pit, and at the bottom lay a terrible decision . . .

"I got a B-plus on my oral report," I heard myself answer. I searched for something else to tell her, the sort of tidbit that would assure her I was doing just fine. "Bob Distefano got up and gave this report he called Five Ways to Get an A."

I knew she would want to hear more, just to keep me talking. "Oh?" she said, pulling onto the expressway. "What did he recommend?"

"First you're supposed to compliment the teacher at the end of class, for making it so interesting. He said teachers scarf up compliments the way a kid gobbles candy. Then he said, 'Now this teacher — he, she, or whatever it is . . .' and that's when Mrs. Tobin said, 'You may resume your seat.' "

"Sounds like one way *not* to get an A," Mom said.

I had exhausted the cheery events of the day,

but luckily the pressure was off me. Rush-hour traffic was fierce, and Mom shifted her attention away from me to concentrate on her driving. I huddled in my coat, trying to keep warm. I couldn't blame the chill on the Chicago weather. It came from inside me.

I wasn't only disappointing myself, I was dragging down our whole class. A hundred times Miss Panova had explained that in any ballet company the weakest dancer brought down the quality of the whole performance. I was no longer a vital member of the team. I was a liability. I couldn't expect the others to tolerate my sloppiness forever.

Elena handled the routine appointments with most of the dialysis patients. Whenever I went to see her, I felt like a prisoner who was out on probation. As long as she felt I was doing well, I could stay out. But if I didn't meet her expectations — if any of my blood tests were out of kilter, or if I showed signs of an infection — she could sentence me to another stay in the hospital. I never felt entirely safe.

At least I was old enough to leave Mom in the waiting room and see Elena by myself. I felt somehow stronger, better able to face the ordeal, knowing she considered me almost grown-up.

My folder lay open on her desk when I came in, and I knew she was studying the latest reports from the lab. My panic rose as she flipped back through the pages, checking, comparing. But at last she looked up and smiled. "You're looking pretty good, Rachel," she said. "Staying on your diet?"

"Yeah," I said. "I'm going to turn into a plate of spaghetti!"

"You feel all right?"

I was about to say the usual — that I was just fine, thanks. But I didn't have to answer Elena the way I answered Mom or Dad or Lici or Miss Panova. Maybe, if I explained, she would have a solution. "I get so sick of medicines and injections and not being able to eat what I want. And I hardly ever feel really *good*, you know what I mean?"

Elena sighed. "Dialysis can only do so much," she said, shaking her head. "At best it's about twenty percent as effective as normally functioning kidneys would be."

"Won't it ever get any better?" I pleaded.

"I think you're still adjusting," Elena said. "But as long as you're on dialysis, you won't feel completely healthy. You have to accept that there'll always be something just not right." She held up her thumb and forefinger, measuring that little sliver of not-rightness that would stay with me.

Suddenly I didn't feel grown-up anymore. I gulped back a lump in my throat and asked, "Can my mom come in now?"

Elena went to the door and called her in a low

voice, as though people were sleeping in the waiting room and couldn't be disturbed. Mom came in and perched on a chair, tense and rigid. It occurred to me that these appointments were an ordeal for her, too. We were enduring it together.

Patiently, Elena went over the details of my latest test results. There was a lot of talk about creatinine levels and something called my BUN. At last she pushed my folder aside and asked, "Do either of you have any other questions?"

"Yes," Mom said abruptly. "What about the transplant list? How long is it going to take?"

"It could happen next week," Elena said. "Or — or it can take a long time. Months. A year. One of the reasons we draw blood is to keep very close tabs on your daughter's antibodies, so that if a kidney comes along, we can try for a good match."

"If I got a transplant, would I feel normal again?" I demanded. "Would I be back to my old self?"

"Look, I can only be honest with you. There is no perfect solution. With a transplant, you have to take medication for the rest of your life. And there's always the chance that your body may reject the organ, you may have to go back on dialysis and wait for another donor. But — " Elena hesitated. "People who undergo a transplant feel much, much better. That's a fact."

*Much, much better!* I had never heard Elena sound so enthusiastic about anything before.

"You're only speaking in terms of a cadaver transplant," Mom said. "According to everything I've been reading, everything people here have told me, the success rate is much higher with a transplant from a live donor."

"The chances for success are greater. But with a cadaver transplant, we see very good results, too, sometimes."

Mom sat very straight. "Rachel's best hope is a kidney from one of her biological relatives," she stated. "She deserves the best possible chance."

"Mrs. Whitaker," Elena said, "we have to work with what we can get. There's still a good possibility — "

"A good possibility, yes!" Mom interrupted. "But not the best! You're saying Rachel has to take something second-rate, just because she's adopted?"

I stared at her. Mom was usually so controlled, as though life were a giant computer keyboard, and if she punched the right buttons the right answer would appear on a cosmic screen. Now she faced a set of questions that had no ready answers. She was threatening to break one of the family rules. It looked to me like she was about to create a scene, right here in Elena's office!

"You can't just write off the idea," she insisted. "Can't the hospital try to contact — her birth mother? Maybe there's a sister or brother, somebody out there who'd be willing to — "

"We cannot force anyone to give up an organ against their will," Elena said. She kept her voice very quiet. "There is no law that obliges a person to go through such a thing. It has to be the individual's free choice. And, in a situation like this — it could open up so many emotions, for all of you. Ethically, the hospital can't get involved in searching for these people and trying to persuade them to donate." She shook her head sadly. "Even though it might be the best thing medically, there are too many other factors to consider."

Mom was silent, but her lips were pressed tight. "The hospital wouldn't have to be involved in the search," she said at last. "There might be other ways."

Elena said nothing. But somewhere in her silence, I felt a secret agreement, as though she and Mom had signed a pact that they would not mention again.

# 7

After class on Monday afternoon, I told Miss Panova what I had decided to do.

She was in the little room off the studio, sorting through some tapes, and at first she didn't notice me when I came in. I stood just inside the door, my heart thudding, hoping that she would glance up at me. But she just searched through the boxes on the table in front of her, until at last I squeezed out, "Miss Panova?"

"Oh, Rachel!" she exclaimed. "Hi. What can I do for you?"

I swallowed. I had lived with my decision for days now, but it didn't seem quite real as long as it only existed in my head. I couldn't bring myself to say the words.

"You wanted to ask me something?" Miss Panova prodded. She didn't have much time. I could hear a crew of kids who had arrived for her beginners' class, scampering around the studio.

"No, it's not exactly a question," I stammered.

"It's more like — something I need to tell you."

She looked straight at me now. Steady and watchful, her eyes forced me to go on. Through the pounding in my ears I said, "I'm going to drop out of ballet."

"What?" Miss Panova stared at me. "How can you? After you've worked so hard, come all this way — "

"I just can't do it," I said past the lump in my throat. "Ever since I got sick, I can't keep up. It just doesn't work."

"But you've been doing quite well," she said, frowning. "I've admired you, sticking with it the way you have. You were back here as soon as you came home from the hospital."

"I know, but — I just get too tired. I'm not — I can't — "

"Look, maybe the advanced class is too demanding for you right now. How about if I switch you to my intermediate group?"

I'd watched the intermediate class once or twice, and I'd seen them perform at recitals. Most of the kids were passable. They had fun dancing. It was something to do after school instead of sitting in front of the TV. But ballet wasn't their passion.

I shook my head. "I don't want to be in any class," I said. "I'd better just — stop."

"But your doctor sent me that note," Miss Panova protested. "She said it was fine for you to dance, she thought it was a good idea for you to keep it up."

"She doesn't understand about ballet," I said miserably. "She just thinks it's like doing exercises. I can *do* it, but I can't do it *well*. And as long as I'm on dialysis, they say I won't feel any better than I do now."

"I hate to see you drop out," Miss Panova said.

I held my breath. If only she would argue with me, insist that I was improving, that she wanted me to stay in her advanced class no matter what. I could still change my mind. I could go back and undo everything I had said . . .

"Maybe you're getting discouraged too easily," Miss Panova began. But she stopped, sighing. "I guess you're the best judge of how you feel. I don't want to pressure you, if you've made a decision."

"I have," I said. I turned away quickly, and hoped she didn't see the tears that slid down my cheeks.

I stumbled out through the studio, past all those third-graders in leotards with their shrill voices and their boundless energy. Lici had gone on ahead of me, and when I reached the bus stop she wasn't there. I waited alone on the bench, empty and numb.

Miss Panova must be relieved. She wouldn't have to make excuses for me anymore. No more stiff little nods of approval, when we both knew I was a disgrace. The advanced class would once again be reserved for her very best pupils.

On my lap I clutched the case with my tights and leotard and my satin toe shoes. They were relics now. They were like old discarded bones from another life.

Had I been too hasty? I might not be on dialysis forever. Elena had said that with a transplant I would feel much, much better. But I couldn't flounder along, waiting for something that might never happen, or might not work even if it happened at last.

I couldn't imagine my life without ballet. I couldn't picture Mondays, Wednesdays, and Fridays without the rush to get to class on time after school. I didn't know what I would do at home without my exercise routines every afternoon. But I had never imagined myself on dialysis, either.

The house was quiet when I unlocked the front door. Monday was Phoebe's Brownies day, so she wouldn't be home until almost five. In a daze I went into the kitchen and opened the refrigerator. It overflowed with forbidden delights — chocolate pudding, peach yogurt, a wedge of cherry pie. Mom tried to cook family dinners that were on my diet, but she couldn't ban tempting snacks from the house. There had to be something here for me. Pushing some cartons and jars aside, I found my after-school snack at last — a bowl of cold steamed noodles.

I cast a furtive glance around the room, as though invisible eyes might be spying on me. Didn't I deserve a treat, after what I'd been through this afternoon? I wouldn't die if I cheated this once. Slowly, cautiously, I lifted the cherry pie from the bottom shelf.

If I was going to cheat, I might as well do it right. I poured myself a tall glass of milk. Then I opened the freezer. Sure enough, there was a quart of vanilla ice cream. It was time I had some cherry pie à la mode.

As I lifted my fork for the first exquisite bite, the telephone rang. They *were* watching me! If I picked up the receiver I would hear Mom's voice, or Elena's, or Dr. Wong's, scolding, "Don't you want to take care of yourself? You have to be more responsible . . ."

The telephone wouldn't be ignored. It rang again, and again. Whoever was on the other end refused to give up. I set down my fork and reached for the receiver. "Hello?"

"Hello, is this Mrs. Whitaker?" It was a woman's voice, distantly friendly, like one of those telemarketers who always called around supper-time with bargains on aluminum siding.

"No," I said warily. "This is her daughter."

"Oh, is this Rachel?" It couldn't be a salesperson. It had to be someone who knew us. And now I detected the faint hiss of long distance on the line.

"Yeah, I'm Rachel," I said. "Who is this?"

"My name is Ms. Winston. I'm returning your mother's call."

"She's at work," I said. "She doesn't get home till five-thirty."

"Oh, that's right. I have a note right here in my card file, with her work number. I'll call her there. Thanks."

In another moment she would hang up, and I would never know who she was or how she knew me. "I'll tell her you called," I promised. "It's Ms. Winston, from — "

"From New England Children's Services. She has my number. Good-bye now."

"'Bye," I echoed.

I set the receiver on its hook. New England Children's Services — the name buzzed through my brain. With utter certainty I knew what it meant.

I had lived in Connecticut until just last year. Wherever I was born, however my adoption was arranged, it must have been in New England somewhere. No wonder Ms. Winston, that anonymous voice on the phone, knew my name. She knew more about me than I did myself — where I came from, how I had been entrusted to a couple named Whitaker. At New England Children's Services, they knew who I was.

Mom had called them. After that talk with Elena last week, I knew the thought of searching for my birth mother was planted in her mind. But she had never told me outright that she intended to make inquiries, and I hadn't dared to ask her. It was as though everything pertaining to my adoption were tucked into a sack and tied up with an impossible knot.

Suddenly I blazed with anger. Who had a better right to know what was going on than I did myself? Why all this cloak-and-dagger business behind my back? I wasn't a baby anymore! I was old enough to understand crucial matters that affected me. It was my life they were whispering about — my past, my future!

On the table beside me, my cherry pie turned soggy in a puddle of melted ice cream. I scraped it into the garbage pail and dropped the dish in the sink. For once, I wasn't the least bit hungry.

I straightened my shoulders and posted myself by the front door. After ten minutes Phoebe breezed in, red-cheeked and full of some story about a Brownie named Lucinda Maxwell, who said she was allergic to licorice jelly beans. I listened, distracted, still waiting.

A car door slammed. I peered between the curtains and spotted Mom's tan Chevy at the end of the front walk. Mom hurried up the steps, bowed under an armload of grocery bags.

"Thanks, Rachel," she said as I opened the door. "Can you take one of these? There — that's better. Careful — that bag has eggs in it."

How could she sound so ordinary, when she had just launched a secret investigation? She followed me into the kitchen and thumped her bags down on the counter, as though nothing unusual had happened since the world started spinning.

"Mom," I said, "you had a phone call."

She opened the freezer and set some cans of orange juice on the shelf. "Did they leave a message?" she asked.

"Yeah. It was a woman from the adoption agency."

Mom shut the freezer and reached into the bag again. She pulled out a package of cheese, but she didn't move to put it away.

"She told me you called her," I said. "She said she'd call you at work." The words came out hard and brittle, like shards of glass.

"Oh, well," Mom said after a moment. "I guess I'll hear from her tomorrow." She turned the cheese over, studying the label, and stepped toward the refrigerator.

"Mom!" I cried. "Tell me what's going on! What did she want?"

"There's nothing to tell you yet. That's why I didn't mention — "

"But you called Connecticut! You talked to those people out there. You're trying to find her, right? My — my — birth mother!"

Slowly Mom pulled out a chair and sat down, facing me. The grocery bags stood on the counter, forgotten. "Your father and I talked it over the other night," Mom said. "We decided we should take the chance — well, just see if there's any information, if there's any remote possibility that your — your birth mother, or some other — biological relative — "

She was laboring over the words, and at last she trailed into helplessness. But I had finally yanked loose the knot, and I couldn't let her tie up the sack again. "You and Dad talked it over," I repeated. "You talked it all over without me! Don't I count? *I'm* who it's all about!"

"We have no idea what we'll find, if we find out anything," Mom said. "These people — who knows what they are? They could be — they could be anything! We didn't want to upset you."

They hadn't set out on purpose to exclude me. I could see that now. Yet still I felt like the victim of a conspiracy, a conspiracy of silence.

"What makes me get upset," I said carefully, "is not being allowed to talk about this stuff. Not knowing. Having to think about it, and guess, all by myself."

Neither of us moved. We sat facing each other across the kitchen table — across a chasm of doubt and apprehension.

"Right now, there's nothing to tell you," Mom said. "I called the agency that arranged your adoption, and of course, the social worker we had is long gone. I talked to this Ms. Winston, and she said she'd see what she could do. And I'll talk to her tomorrow."

"And will you tell me what she says?" I asked.

"If you really want to know — yes, all right. I'll tell you."

Mom got to her feet, brushing her hair back from her forehead. She picked up the cheese again and stowed it where it belonged. For the moment, the subject of adoption was closed. Only for the moment.

# 8

I can't claim that our discussion that afternoon
brought the topic of my adoption totally out
into the open. Whenever the subject came up, Dad
still went silent and strange or quietly walked out
of the room. But my mother kept her word. She
kept me abreast of all the latest developments in
what we came to call "The Case." The trouble was
nothing ever happened.

"I talked to that social worker again, that Ms.
Winston," she informed me the next afternoon.
"She says she'd like to help us and she'll do what
she can, but it'll take time."

"How much time?"

"Time. She didn't say how much of it."

"Does she know my birth mother's name? Does
she have her address?"

"She couldn't say."

"What do you mean she couldn't — "

"She said it's confidential. She has to speak with
her supervisor. We'll talk again next week."

A week later: "Ms. Winston's supervisor gave her permission to tell us they found your birth mother's name in the records."

"Oh! What is it?"

"She's not allowed to tell us what it is. She can only say that they know."

"And do they know where she is?"

"Ms. Winston says she's out of state."

"You mean out of Connecticut? So what?"

"It will take time, she says."

"How long?"

"Time."

My birth mother, that mysterious person who was so irrevocably connected to me, was somewhere "out of state." I pictured a United States map, the kind that rolls down in front of a blackboard. In my mind's eye, a pointer glided across it, over green plains and blue mountain ranges, to vanish somewhere beyond the paper, off the edge of the known world.

The search became part of our lives, a slow, steady undercurrent that ran through everything we did and said at home. But whenever Mom and I talked about the latest tidbit from Ms. Winston, we didn't dare to guess aloud what we might discover if the searching came to an end.

I told Lici about The Case after the third message from Ms. Winston, the one which said New England Children's Services had to send some forms for Mom and Dad to sign. It was a blustery afternoon in late November — a Tuesday, so Lici had no ballet class. A little cautiously I invited her to come over after school, not quite sure what we could find to talk about. We sat in the living room with a bowl of salt-free crackers between us, crunching instead of talking. Lici was the very essence of tact. She was careful not to mention Miss Panova's class. I longed to hear about everything they were doing, their plans for the next recital, even Joy's latest dressing-room story. But if I let Lici begin, I might break into tears and embarrass us both.

In the aquarium under the window, a pair of angelfish swooped and glided. I let my thoughts drift into their world with its china castle and carpet of colored stones.

Beside me, Lici shifted uneasily. She cleared her throat, a polite warning that she really couldn't stay long.

"You know what?" I blurted. "They're trying to find my mother." From the look of amazement which flashed across her face, I knew that she knew which mother I meant.

"Who is?" she demanded, leaning toward me in excitement. "Why are they looking? How will they know where she is?"

She listened, enthralled, as I explained the details. "Wow! That's neat!" she exclaimed when I finished. "You'll finally *know*, after all this time!"

"Well, yeah," I said. "But *what* will I know? That's the real question."

"She might be somebody fantastic," Lici said. "Hey, maybe you've even got a bunch of brothers and sisters you never knew about! You could go visit them in the summer."

"On a farm," I said, letting myself get into the spirit. "They'll raise horses and goats and — and bees for honey. And they'll live in this big old rambling house with a rooster weather vane on the roof."

"Oh, I was thinking of New York," Lici said. "What if your mother's an actress on Broadway? And your big brother, he's this high-powered agent for theater people and dancers. Your family has a penthouse apartment and a butler who greets you at the door, and besides that they have a couple of getaways like in Hawaii and Bermuda and Miami Beach."

"If they've got all that, they're not going to be exactly thrilled when a poor relation like me turns up. I think I'd rather have them be — a little more ordinary. The farm would be okay."

"But maybe they'll be the kind of people who can advance your career," Lici said. "I mean, after you have the transplant, you'll start dancing again, right? Maybe — "

"I just can't think that far ahead." I pleaded with her to understand. "They might not want anything to do with me. There's got to be a reason why they put me up for adoption. They didn't want me when I was born, so why should they want me now? And then — what we've got to ask for — would you have an operation and let them cut out part of your insides, to help a total stranger?"

I needed to talk about all this, I realized suddenly. Even Mom couldn't speak of anything except the logistics of the search — and there was so much, much more pounding through my head day after day. There were so many questions I hadn't been able to share with anyone.

Lici was silent. For the first time, I think, she understood how complicated my situation was. But in a few moments she rallied, ready to paint it with the brightest colors she could find. "I bet when you were born, your birth mother didn't want to give you up. Maybe she just didn't have a choice. She was poor — or sick — or — " She trailed off. The lights of Broadway were fading fast.

"Or locked up in jail?" I suggested. "She might be an ax murderer."

"Come on, mothers don't do stuff like that. You keep looking on the worst side."

"I can't help it. I get these awful pictures in my head sometimes! I don't know where they come from."

"Chances are it was a teenage pregnancy," Lici said. "No prisons or anything dramatic."

"You mean like that film we had last week in health ed?" It had been full of dire warnings about struggling young girls with babies, dropping out of school, searching hopelessly for jobs, standing on welfare lines. The babies cried a lot, and the girls had big circles under their eyes and never smiled. From the movie, you would never figure out how such a tragedy could occur. You got the definite impression that rock music and slow dancing were to blame.

"If she were grown-up, she probably would have kept you," Lici went on. "She could have worked, or gotten married or something, don't you think?"

"Think?" I repeated. "I don't begin to know what I think."

The wind flung a rattling handful of sleet at the window. The cold crept in even through the weather stripping Dad had tacked over the cracks, and I huddled against the cushions. I tried to fasten the word *mother* to my picture of a scared, desperate kid barely older than I was myself. How could I crash back into her world now, after all these years? How could I expect her to go through pain and even danger in order to help me? Somewhere, in that unknown place off the edge of the map, she might still be wishing I had never been born. She might think of me as the creature that had ruined her life forever.

"It's not that easy, is it?" Lici said. "When you first told me they were looking, I thought it was kind of like a game."

"I wish it was. And I wish I could quit playing any time I want."

Lici bit her lip and gazed at the circling angelfish. "Then you really don't want to find out who your mother is?"

I didn't answer at first. I sat still, trying to absorb what she had said. I wondered how I would feel if Ms. Winston called some afternoon to inform us that they were terribly sorry, my birth mother simply could not be located, and New England Children's Services was giving up the search. I tried on the feelings that might sweep through me at the news — disappointment? relief? anger? They would all tangle together, and I wouldn't know whether to laugh or cry or shout with rage. But afterward . . . I knew what would be left — a gaping hole at the very center of my being.

"It doesn't make any difference whether I *want* to know or not," I said at last. "Now that we've gotten this far, and I'm thinking about it all the time — I guess I *have* to know."

# 9

I hated to go home after school. Maybe it was the long walk to the bus, with the wind whipping my face and my hands going numb even in my wool gloves. Maybe it was walking up our dark, silent street, the houses all shut tight against the winter and the people huddled inside trying to stay warm.

Once I reached home, the real ordeal began. I dreaded Mom's anxious questions: "How are you feeling, Rachel? . . . Are you tired? . . . No headaches today? . . . What did you eat for lunch? . . ." I dreaded the bleak emptiness when there was no word from New England Children's Services, and the shivering uncertainty on those rare days when Ms. Winston called with a message. And always, controlling whatever I did, loomed my dialysis schedule. I could never escape my treatments. The treatments that kept me alive. The treatments that kept me a prisoner.

I knew I should feel grateful. I woke every

morning to a fresh day, free to walk and laugh and rush downstairs to breakfast. Everyone was working so hard to keep me alive — Dr. Wong and Elena, and of course my parents. Mom and Dad never mentioned it in my presence, but I'd overheard them worrying together about how much our insurance might not cover. And the money was only one small piece of their troubles. I was always on their minds — how I was doing, what the lab said about my blood chemistry, what would become of me. When I grumbled and complained, Dad tried to joke me into a cheerful mood, and Mom assured me that things would get better soon. In front of me they were unflaggingly pleasant, as though I would splinter into bits if they dared to lose patience with me. But they snapped at Phoebe when she dawdled over her homework or left her boots in the middle of the floor, and sometimes late at night I heard their voices raised high and tense from the bedroom down the hall.

I was the source of all the tension in our house. It spread out from me like the maze of cracks in the windshield of Dad's car that day some kid hit it with a stone. That was really why I hated to go home after school.

More and more often, I wandered aimlessly through the halls after the final bell rang. When the cheering squad practiced, I'd hang around the gym, listening to the chorus of "Go, Hornets, go!" and watching the twirlers bounce into formation.

Sometimes I went up to the science room and gazed at Mr. Ciardi's shelf of specimens — a jar of pickled squids, displays of seashells and minerals and a chunk of Hawaiian lava. He even had a grinning human skull with desolate, hollow eyes. Some afternoons I sat in the school library until it closed, losing myself in books about the Amazon jungles and people of the South Seas.

It was in the library that I met Melanie Kim. Actually, I'd been seeing her all year long — we were in the same class, after all. She sat behind me in English, but we'd never exchanged a word unless it was to pass a stack of test papers down the row. Melanie made a career of being quiet. I think if a tornado ripped the roof off the school and left us staring up at the sky, she would have sat silently, studying the damage and carefully deciding what needed to be done.

I was sitting in the library, poring over a book about Balinese dancers, when a voice said softly, "I wish I could draw."

I looked up, and there was Melanie across the table from me. She had sat down so silently I never even heard her pull out a chair. "Why?" I asked. "What do you want to draw for?"

"I need a design for the cover of the yearbook."

At our school, the yearbook was a big thing with the eighth-graders. A lot of them had been together since kindergarten, and they would be scattered to high schools all over the city next year. The yearbook would store up a lot of their important memories. I hadn't paid much attention to all the talk about the class will, and the elections for "Most likely to succeed" and "Most inseparable friends" and "Best dresser." I had only been around for a year, and besides, I'd been busy with ballet most of that time. When they asked for volunteers to work on the yearbook committee, it never occurred to me to raise my hand.

Apparently Melanie Kim had raised hers. "Why are you the one who has to design it?" I asked. "There must be other people on the committee who are good in art."

Melanie shook her head. "There were. Miriam Claudio was going to do it, till she moved away. And then Lori Daniels promised that she would. But she got two D's on her report card, and now her father's making her quit all her extracurriculars till she gets her grades up."

I never imagined that Melanie could string so many sentences together at once. I was so startled that, before I could think it through, I found myself saying, "I can draw — a little."

"You can?" She slid a pad of paper and a pencil toward me and sat back to wait. She reminded me of Zila Mae back in the hospital.

For a few seconds I hesitated, the pencil poised over the clean, white sheet. Then, swiftly, before I had time to think how peculiar it might seem, I sketched a dancing girl with bells on her wrists and ankles, and a headdress of plumes and flowers. She looked a lot like one of the girls in the book I had been reading, but I posed her in a *plié*.

Wordlessly I pushed the pad back to Melanie's side of the table. She looked at it for a long moment, and met my gaze with a smile. "I like that," she said. "You could do a cover, I bet."

"I don't know anything about it, really," I stammered. "I don't study art, or anything like that. I just draw for fun, when there's nothing else to do."

"It can be anything that shows what school is like," Melanie said. "You can use four colors. But we need it by next Tuesday."

"Wait a minute," I protested. "I didn't say I'd do it. I was just curious, that's all."

"Well, *can* you? Are you moving? Did you get any D's on your report card?"

I never knew that a quiet person could be so forceful. She acted as though I were under moral obligation to design her cover unless I could produce a proper excuse. I thought of tossing out that I had Henoch Schonlein purpura. That ought to meet the requirements.

Even if she didn't know the name of my disease, Melanie must have heard about what I'd been through. I had a certain notoriety at school, being the only girl in the eighth grade who had ever been rushed to the hospital with her life hanging by a thread. Everyone knew my name now. They had a tag to fasten on me — I was Rachel who almost died, Rachel who survived thanks to a mysterious and rather nasty treatment. Rachel who couldn't pee.

Ever since I stopped dancing, I had gone along with that definition of myself. Kidney disease was the center of my life, stretching into everything I did. But Melanie Kim behaved as if she hadn't heard the news.

"Okay," I said. "I guess I'll give it a try."

Melanie's eyes sparkled as though I'd just handed her a winning lottery ticket. "I'm sure glad I ran into you!" she exclaimed. "I didn't know what I'd do. You saved my life."

Apparently my idea of saving a life wasn't quite the same as hers. "I haven't done anything yet," I reminded her. "What if I really mess up? I might hand you something that's totally the pits."

"You won't," Melanie assured me. "It'll be just what we need."

"By Tuesday?" I repeated, dazed.

"By Tuesday."

All the way home on the bus, my mind was full of images of school. In four colors, blackboards and notebooks, gym suits and cafeteria trays and backpacks arranged and rearranged themselves inside my head. I imagined a collage of kids' faces, smiling or serious, frowning in concentration or glinting with mischief. Perhaps I should draw a picture of the school itself. But no, it was an ugly building, flat and straight as a box. I would have to think some more. Sooner or later I would hit on something.

I wondered what Melanie was like, besides being a dedicated member of the yearbook committee. She had a lot of power concealed behind her quiet veneer. It might be interesting to find out who she *really* was.

Mom's car was just pulling up as I unlocked the front door. "Hi, Rachel," she called, hurrying up the sidewalk. "What kind of a day's it been?"

"Pretty good!" I said, and ran up to my room to find some poster paper.

# 10

"**H**ello, is your mother home?"
My heart lurched. I knew that distant, friendly voice, even before it went on to explain, "This is Ms. Winston, from New England Children's Services."

"She's still at work," I managed. "May I take a message?"

Ms. Winston hesitated. Maybe her supervisor hadn't given her permission to speak to me directly.

"Oh, I should have tried her work number first," Ms. Winston scolded herself. "Let me make a note about that."

"May I take a message?" I repeated.

"Well . . ." I held my breath. Now, as I stood alone in the kitchen, now the truth would burst upon me . . .

"All right," Ms. Winston decided at last. "Just tell her we received the forms, and everything is in order. We can move forward with the investigation."

Move forward? An inchworm moved forward. So did a glacier. How long was this investigation process going to take? I knew the answer. It would take time.

Any news from New England Children's Services — even non-news like this — always left me feeling weak and shaky. For a few minutes I just sat at the table, too confused to know what I wanted to do next. Finally I wandered out to the living room. My picture for the yearbook lay on the coffee table, where I was sure to remember it when I packed my things for school tomorrow.

Not that I was likely to forget it. I'd worked on it all weekend. My room was littered with false starts — crumpled collages, faces ripped in two, a laborious abstract design that looked like a kindergartener's attempt with finger paints. Somewhere around Try Number Six I drew a pyramid of books in the middle of the sheet, but I tossed it aside — not enough life to it — and plunged on. Still, by Try Number Fourteen or Fifteen, I picked it up again, and found myself doodling around the edges. Before I knew I had an idea, I had sketched in two faces, one on each side, bending toward each other over the pile. The boy's face was wrinkled with dismay, but the girl laughed reassuringly.

I couldn't say exactly what was happening in

the scene. Maybe the boy was upset because he had to learn everything that was in all those volumes, and the girl was telling him it would be a snap. Or perhaps he was anxious because the books were about to topple over onto the floor, while she was looking forward to the crash. Whatever their story, they seemed somehow to be typical kids at school, struggling to make sense of it all, but managing to have fun at the same time.

I took the picture from the coffee table and turned it from side to side, admiring it from every angle. I couldn't quite believe I had done it myself. Where had the idea come from, anyway? However I did it, the picture was finished, and I was sure that Melanie would like it. I liked it myself, and I was hard to please.

Phoebe and Mom arrived almost together. While Phoebe stormed around, searching for a missing homework assignment, I explained to Mom about Ms. Winston's call.

"Sometimes I wonder if there's another way to go about this," she said, sighing. "By the time they crack The Case, you'll be applying to college."

Mom went into the kitchen and began clattering pots and pans. "A little bit of veal won't hurt you," she decided. "I thought I'd try something fancy tonight, since we're having company."

"We are? Who's coming?"

Mom looked up, startled. "Kathy Wheeling. You know, Karen's niece. I've mentioned Karen — she's the head programmer in my department. I thought I told you Kathy was coming."

"No. You didn't." I watched her with a vague suspicion. "What is Karen's niece coming for?"

"You might like to meet her. She's a junior at Northwestern, very interesting — and — she's on CAPD, too."

"Mom!" I exploded. "Why don't you tell me these things ahead of time? What's the big secret?"

"Well," she admitted, "I was afraid you wouldn't want to meet her. I'm not always sure how you'll react."

"How *should* I react?" I demanded. "It sounds like a terrific evening. We can talk about lab tests and diets and injections — all that neat stuff."

"It might be good for you," Mom said firmly, "to realize you're not the only one this has ever happened to."

"Yeah. Misery loves company." Why did she have to remind me about illness and treatments all the time? Couldn't she let me spend a few hours as though nothing were wrong with me? That had been part of the joy of working on the yearbook cover. It gave me the chance to think about all of the ordinary pieces of my life, the things that had never changed even after I got sick. Why did Mom have to walk in and break my mood with Kathy Wheeling?

"She's going out of her way to spend an evening with you," Mom said. "You can at least make an effort to be pleasant."

Her words stung. She had been treating me like a Tiffany chandelier for so long now, I had begun to feel that I had license to say whatever popped into my head. My life was rotten, so the rules of courtesy no longer applied.

Even if her efforts were clumsy sometimes, Mom sincerely wanted to help. I owed my life to her and Dad and the people at the hospital. At the rate I was going, they might begin to wonder whether I was worth the trouble.

"I'll be nice," I promised. "I'll probably think of some questions I want to ask her."

Kathy Wheeling was late. By the time she finally arrived, Dad was grumbling about the prospect of starvation, and Phoebe had eaten up most of the hors d'oeuvres. It almost looked as though I would be spared the evening's ordeal, when the doorbell rang.

Phoebe loved to meet new people. She rushed for the door, tangled her foot in a throw rug, and nearly went sprawling. But she managed to fling herself upright again, all flailing arms and legs, and was the first to welcome Kathy Wheeling.

Flushed with the wind and stammering apologies, Kathy shed her coat and scarf, boots and mittens. She was slender and dainty, with curly dark hair tumbling to her shoulders. "Are you Rachel?" she asked Phoebe.

"Yeah," Phoebe said, grinning. She pointed to me. "This is my sister Phoebe."

If Phoebe wanted to pretend she was me, I would play right along. I could stay in the background and let her ask the questions, let her tell the stories about nurses and needles. It didn't make much sense that anyone would want to trade places with me, but Phoebe didn't always obey the rules of logic.

"Hi, Rachel," Kathy said, taking Phoebe's hand warmly. "My aunt's been telling me all about you."

"Oh, yeah?" Phoebe said, beaming. "Like what'd she say?" Gleefully she bounced on her toes. It was the attention, I realized in a flash. Phoebe was hungry for attention. These days I hogged it all.

"Phoebe," Mom exclaimed, hurrying forward. "What are you up to now?"

Phoebe giggled and dropped Kathy's hand. Bewildered, Kathy gazed from Phoebe to Mom, and over to me. "Wait a second," she said. She gave me a long, studying look, and broke out laughing. "*You're* Rachel! I *thought* Aunt Karen said you were older. You almost fooled me that time!"

We all laughed, a little nervously, but even nervous laughter was better than the strained silence I had expected. Dad emerged from the den, and after we stood around for a while chatting about the chance of snow tonight, Mom ushered us into the dining room.

Food has a wonderful way of loosening up conversation. As the serving dishes made their rounds, Mom asked Kathy how she liked Northwestern. She liked it a lot, she said, even though the classes were tough. She was majoring in journalism, and a few questions from Dad brought out the fact that she was writing an article about insurance fraud. She and Dad launched into a spirited debate that didn't wind down until we cleared away the dessert dishes.

As they talked, I studied Kathy from across the table. I liked her smile. It was cautious at first, but soon it lit up her whole face. She leaned forward, her voice rising with excitement. Her cheeks wore a healthy flush, her eyes sparkled. Maybe Mom had the story wrong. It was hard to imagine Kathy down with the flu, let alone surviving on CAPD.

When I picked up my empty dish, Kathy followed me out to the kitchen. "Oh, you girls don't need to help," Mom said quickly. "Go in the other room and visit."

No, I wanted to protest, we have nothing to say to each other! But another part of me was bursting with questions. I wanted — needed —

94

Kathy's whole story, from its beginning straight to this very moment.

"Okay," Kathy said. She winked at me. "You *are* Rachel, aren't you?"

"I was this morning," I said, and we were both giggling as we went out to the den.

Once we were settled on the couch, though, I didn't know where to start. I might have sat there like a lump all night, but Kathy plunged right in. "Your mom told my aunt you're waiting for a kidney transplant," she said. "I had one for three years. It was great."

"Only three years!" I exclaimed. "It didn't last?"

"My first one rejected, but I'm waiting for another one," Kathy said. "I'm back on CAPD for now."

"Doesn't that really bum you out?" I asked. "After all that, you're back where you started."

She nodded, silent for a pained moment. Maybe she didn't want to talk about it, and I had pushed her too far. "The thing was," she said at last, "I had those three good years. I know it can work. The first time I had a cadaver transplant. You know how they do this tissue typing, to try to find a good match in your family?" I didn't know, since the issue had never really come up in my case, but I let her go on. "The best match they found that time was my brother, and he was only twelve. I didn't want him to donate, even if the doctors

95

would have let him. He was too little, it wouldn't be fair. So I ended up with a cadaver transplant, like I said. That was when I was fifteen."

"It sounds so creepy — a cadaver transplant," I said. "Didn't it make you feel weird?"

She pushed back her hair from her forehead, remembering. "I thought about it a lot at first. I kept wondering about the person — the donor. They told me it was a twenty-two-year-old woman who died in a car crash. Sometimes I'd think, wow, if she hadn't died, I'd still be on dialysis. And was it fair for me to benefit from the awful thing that happened to some total stranger?"

We were both quiet for a little while. Phoebe's voice drifted in from the living room, asking Dad to help her study for her spelling test. "But then I had a long talk with the social worker at the hospital," Kathy continued. "She was a real neat lady. And she told me the family of the woman was so pleased that she had been accepted as a donor. They felt like in some way a part of her was still alive, helping someone else. It gave them something to hold onto through the worst time."

"But then that kidney was rejected." It sounded so grim. Suppose I had a transplant and, after all the waiting and hoping, the same thing happened to me!

"Yeah, it did eventually. That can happen."

"So you went back on dialysis?"

"You got it. Two and a half years now."

"Two and a half years!" I burst out. "How do you stand it? I'll go crazy if I have to stay on it that long!"

"It gets easier after a while," Kathy said. "I guess I'm used to it. By now it's just part of the routine."

"Like brushing your teeth?" I asked bitterly.

"Well, maybe not quite like that — but still, it's just something you have to do. So you do it and get on with things."

"What things?" I demanded. "I can do stuff that doesn't take a lot of energy. Schoolwork, and drawing, things like that. But I can't dance anymore. That's what I miss most."

Kathy frowned. "Why can't you dance?" she asked. "You mean your doctor won't let you? I never heard of — "

"Oh, she said I could. It's not that. It's just — I can't do all of the things I used to. I'm just not very good now. So what's the use?"

Kathy cupped her chin in her hand. "Do you think you gave up too soon?" she asked. "Maybe if you kept at it a while, you'd work your way back into it. You've only been on CAPD for a couple of months, right?"

I nodded. "I'll never be really good, as long as I'm on dialysis. It takes too much out of me."

"You might change your mind," Kathy said. "At some point, you might be ready to try again. After a while, you learn how far you can push yourself.

Sometimes it's like rowing upstream. But I always figure it's worth whatever it takes, to do the things that are important to you."

I would never discover Kathy's secret. I would never become so calm and relaxed about dialysis, or look so pleased with life.

"My brother wants to donate for me," she was saying. "We've got to wait till he's at least eighteen, but that's less than a year away. Even then . . ." She paused. "Even then, it's such a big decision. I'm doing okay on treatments now, I'm not sure I want him to go through with it."

"Why not?"

"For one thing, what if something happens to his other kidney? He'd wind up on dialysis himself. But besides that, it's such a huge responsibility. If someone you know gives you part of themselves, out of love, you'd really feel you have to do something with your life."

"Kind of like they own a share in you?" I asked, laughing a little.

"Well, not exactly. I mean, my brother's not like that. But I'd feel like I should make my life really count somehow. I'd want to give something back."

I hadn't thought of that part before. I'd never gotten much beyond myself — my squeamishness about having someone else's organ, my eagerness to get off CAPD, my longing to dance again. Now I began to realize what a transplant truly meant, the awesome power of that gift of life.

"Is it worth it?" I asked. "When you had your transplant before, did you really feel that good?"

Kathy stretched her arms wide, as if she wanted to embrace the whole world. "I felt brand-new," she said. "I felt — I just can't tell you — so very much, much better!"

# 11

Sometimes Mom complained that the only reward for doing a good job is more work. I never knew what she meant until I handed Melanie my design for the cover of the yearbook. "I *like* this!" she exclaimed. "It's different." She said "different" as though it were a high compliment.

Melanie looked at the picture for a long moment and rolled it back into its cardboard tube. "We could really use your help with some of the inside layout," she said with her most winning smile. "Could you come to our meeting this afternoon, in Miss Perlman's room?"

We weren't moving away. I hadn't gotten any D's on my report card. How could I say no?

I had enjoyed working on the cover, and I went to the meeting, looking forward to another interesting assignment. But I didn't think the meeting itself would be much fun. I pictured a lot of serious-minded kids like Melanie hunched over stacks of papers, or maybe sorting index cards into alphabetical order. I would have preferred to go anywhere else, if I had anywhere else to go.

Miss Perlman's room seemed almost empty when I peered in. I was backing away, convinced I was in the wrong spot, when a grinning boy not much taller than I was ambushed me from behind the half-open door. "We've got another one!" he shouted. "Hold still! You're not getting away!"

Melanie and another girl crowded into the doorway. "Oh, Rachel," Melanie cried. "You're here! Come on in. We need you."

"Yeah, quick, before you change your mind," the boy said. "This meeting is a complete bust. We've got more deserters than troops."

Miss Perlman, the yearbook's faculty adviser, presided over an echoing room full of empty desks and chairs. "Well," she said cheerfully, "four sets of hands are a lot better than none. Consider yourselves a very elite group. Sort of a secret society."

"The password is *peanut butter*," said the boy, whose name was Chip. "And the response is — "

"Jelly!" Melanie cried, and we were off.

I couldn't really call it work. Any time we threatened to become serious, Chip would toss out a crazy remark, or put on an exaggerated, sober frown that set us all giggling. Apparently today was a momentous occasion, as the class pictures had come in at last. In the group picture of Mrs. Harrison's second grade, I spotted one little girl with two fingers in the air, putting bunny ears on the head of the boy in front of her. Miss Perlman sighed and said we would have to instruct the printers to white it out, but the other girl, Gloria, said no, we should leave it alone, it was so totally second grade. Miss Perlman finally shrugged and flipped to the next class.

Besides the big group pictures of every class, the yearbook would include individual shots of each of us eighth-graders. Gloria put her hands over her face when she saw hers — it was taken way back in September, she wailed, back when her hair was all chopped off and ugly! "Doesn't this secret society have any clout?" she demanded. "Can't we ink in a ponytail or something?"

Melanie passed me a handful of pictures, and I rippled through them until I stared into my own face. There was last September's me, smiling quietly as if I had some private joke. I searched in vain for some hint of trouble, some foreboding of the calamity that lay in wait for me only weeks after that shot was taken. My life had been so smooth back then. I ate whatever I wanted. If I was thirsty, I could take a long refreshing drink at the water fountain. I was a stranger to needles and tubes — and I was a dancer.

"Now comes the fun part," Miss Perlman announced. "Now you can pick out the candid shots."

"Funniest Home Videos," Gloria chortled. "These better be good!"

One by one, Miss Perlman handed the photos

around. First came a couple of fifth-graders, look-ing very proud in scaly green alligator costumes for their class play. The next one got everybody giggling — Mr. Ciardi, gazing into a test tube with the grin of a mad scientist. There was a kin-dergarten boy with chocolate ice cream from ear to ear, and a rather blurry picture of Oscar the janitor waving a broom around as if he were con-ducting an orchestra. Somehow the pictures got funnier and funnier. Even the ones that were too dark or out of focus made us all howl with laugh-ter.

Where had I been that week in October, when students and teachers were roaming the halls with cameras, ready to snap the unsuspecting? I didn't even remember hearing about the "Candid Shots" page in the yearbook before. In October I was just out of the hospital. Having moved from Con-necticut in the middle of seventh grade, and miss-ing two weeks so near the start of this school year, I had never gotten very involved in school life. And of course, I had poured most of my energy into ballet. I put in six hours at school every day, but I had always remained detached from the peo-ple I met there.

Eventually we calmed down enough to argue which were the dozen best photos, sifting through a stack an inch thick. It was four-thirty before we reached an uneasy consensus. Even then Chip muttered mutiny because no one else voted for his favorite — a really gross lunchroom scene with a couple of boys slinging pizza. "That's the trouble with girls," he pouted. "You people got no taste."

"Next week," Miss Perlman broke in, "we've got even more fun to look forward to. We've got to go over the eighth-grade Class Will."

"You mean the eighth-grade Class Won't," Chip said, and we were all laughing again.

The meeting really *had* been fun, I admitted to myself as I headed for the bus stop. I couldn't remember the last time I had laughed so hard, or enjoyed being with a group of people so much. And I could spend another afternoon with the Secret Society next week. We could put together the Class Won't.

By the time I got home, Mom's car was already parked out front. I breezed through the door and tossed my books onto a chair. "I'm home," I called, kicking off my boots. "Where is everybody?"

"Rachel." I heard a strange note of tension in Mom's voice. The sound of my name rang with news — stunning news — and I guessed without another word what it had to be.

I stood motionless, my coat hanging over one arm, as Mom moved toward me across the dining room. "They called, didn't they?" I said as she drew nearer. "New England Children's Services."

"Yes, Ms. Winston called," Mom said. She leaned against the back of a chair, as though her legs would no longer hold her up.

The question was so simple, but I struggled to get the words out. "Did they find her?"

The answer was simple, too, but I waited through a long thick silence before Mom finally said, "Yes."

My coat slid to a heap at my feet. We stared at each other while I tried to take in what she had just told me. My mother was real. She existed, not out there beyond the edge of the map, but in an actual location somewhere — somewhere with an address, a telephone. She had a name. Perhaps Ms. Winston had spoken to her, had told her about me . . .

"They found out where she's living," Mom said, echoing my thoughts. "They traced her through the place where she works somehow."

Suddenly I was ablaze with questions. "Where *does* she live? What kind of job has she got? How old is she? Is she short like me? Is she — "

"Ms. Winston couldn't tell me," Mom said. "She claims passing any information at this stage would be a breach of confidence."

"Breach of confidence!" I exploded. "What's she protecting her from? She's got to give us the phone number, at least, so we can call her up."

"Hearing from us out of the blue could be an awful shock for her," Mom pointed out. "And what we're asking — it's not a small thing. Who knows how she may react."

The room swayed around me. I dropped onto the couch. "Ms. Winston knows all about her, and she won't tell? It's not fair! She has to let us know what she found out!"

Mom shook her head. "Ms. Winston contacted her, and explained our situation. She says your — your birth mother wants some time to think. Ms. Winston gave her our number, and it's up to her to call us."

"You mean, she might just decide not to, and that's that? We'll wait and wait and never hear from her — "

"We don't know that will happen. She might call tomorrow."

" — and I'll be stuck on dialysis for the rest of my life," I rushed on, barely listening. "I should never have hoped for a transplant! I shouldn't have even thought about it!"

"Rachel, calm down." Mom could be maddeningly rational. "Whether or not it comes from someone in your birth family, you *will* have a transplant. You *won't* be on dialysis forever, you know that."

"But the waiting list is so long! I can't stand it!"

"It may not be much longer now."

"And if I get one of those cadaver transplants, it might not work. It didn't work for Kathy Wheeling."

Mom covered her face with her hands. Her

shoulders shook. If she starts to cry, I thought, it will be like the whole house caving in. I'll feel like I'm buried alive! In that moment, I would have given anything to hear her being maddeningly rational once more.

At last Mom lowered her hands to her sides, composed again. "It's going to work out," she promised. "I don't know what will happen, but when this is over, everything will be all right."

She wasn't maddeningly rational now. Reason had deserted her completely. If I had learned anything these past months, it was that there were no guarantees. Health, security, life itself could be snatched away from you on a whim of fate.

But if Mom still believed so fervently in her promise, I could hang onto my own hopes a bit longer. A time still might come when I would feel supple and strong again, and sail through the day without ever having to think about my body.

"But *when* will this be over?" I couldn't resist asking. "When is everything going to start being all right?"

"We can't know that," Mom said. "Waiting for a phone call, for your name to come up on the transplant list — it can all take a while."

"How long?" I demanded.

She shrugged and managed a shaky little laugh. "You know and I know. Time."

# 12

I saw her as I waited for the Milwaukee Avenue bus the next afternoon. Ancient and lost, she shambled toward me down the sidewalk, tangles of matted brown hair escaping through a tear in her dirty scarf. From each hand dragged a cluster of bulging shopping bags, like grotesquely swollen bunches of grapes.

For a moment she turned to study a store window across the street, and I thought she might drift away. But no — she set off again, aiming straight for the bench where I sat.

"Pardon me," she said, and her voice was surprisingly light and clear. "Can you please tell me what time the bus arrives?"

"I don't think there's any schedule," I said. "It just comes when it gets here."

She fumbled in a coat pocket and brought out a child's wristwatch with a broken strap. She gazed at it, frowning. "I don't want to be delayed," she said. "I have a very important appointment with my agent."

It hurt to watch her, but I couldn't tear my eyes away. She was younger than she appeared at first. Her face was actually smooth, and her hands were unwrinkled beneath the layers of grime. Instead of seventy, she might be only thirty-five. Young enough . . .

I slid to the far end of the bench as she prepared to sit down. Getting settled was a laborious process for her, involving endless arrangements and rearrangements of her shopping bags. A high-heeled shoe tumbled out, and a battered saucepan clattered to the ground. As she scrambled to retrieve them, a pile of old 45 RPM records spilled from another bag onto the pavement. "My agent will kill me if I'm late," she muttered. "I've got to be there."

She was still on her hands and knees, stuffing things into her floppy plastic bags, when the bus wheezed up to the curb. She half rose, only to shake her head and drop to the ground again. "No!" she said fiercely. "Not that driver! He insulted me! Called me a disturbance."

"Come on," I heard myself shout to her as I clambered up the steps. "Hurry up." But she did not move.

I slipped into a seat and craned my neck to watch her as the bus pulled away. As she disappeared from view, still squatting among her bags, the thought stabbed through me: *She might be my mother!*

I had no way of knowing, after all. I only knew that my birth mother had left Connecticut. She might be in Albuquerque, or Seattle, or Juneau, Alaska — so why not Chicago? She might be any woman in her late twenties, or thirties, or forties. She might be crouched on the sidewalk this minute, with her whole life in her plastic shopping bags.

It wasn't fair! Wasn't it bad enough having kidney disease, being on dialysis, without having a bag lady for a mother? How could I accept a kidney from her? How could I tie my own life up to someone like that?

I was being ridiculous. The chances that I would ever run into my birth mother were one in a hundred million.

My gaze roved over the other passengers. Ahead of me, two women chattered in Polish, but they were old enough to be grandmothers. The woman across the aisle looked the right age, but I could safely rule her out — she was Chinese. Twisting in my seat, I studied the people behind me, and I saw her again.

This time she wore a nurse's uniform with a starched white cap. Hands folded on her lap, she smiled quietly to herself, deep in her own thoughts. Most people on the bus fidgeted, looked out the window, studied their watches or the ads on the ceiling — but she was still and calm.

I imagined her on a hospital ward. Other nurses were always rushing, always telling you to hurry, or scolding you to relax. Some fluttered around with jangling small talk that was supposed to cheer you up. But this nurse, she would carry peace and assurance with her from room to room. She would always have time, and she would choose her words carefully to make certain they were the right ones.

I wished she had been there when I was in the hospital. I wished I had known her all my life, from the very beginning.

She never seemed to notice that I was watching her. At the next stop she rose and descended from the rear door. On the sidewalk she whisked off her cap, and I saw that her hair was a soft honey brown, not like mine at all. That didn't mean anything, of course. Anyone could have a carrot-top child.

As the bus waited at the light, she disappeared around the corner without a backward glance. For a few moments she left me strangely empty and abandoned, as though I really belonged to her and she had turned away without a flicker of recognition.

The next time I spotted my mother, Mom and Phoebe and I were out at the Woodfield Mall. Phoebe was swooning with boredom as Mom and I searched through rack after rack of spring jackets. She ducked between the racks, popping out at us from unexpected hiding places among the trailing coats. Once or twice Mom ordered her to cut it out, and Phoebe emerged with a long-suffering sigh to mope along beside us. But she always slipped back into her game, and after a while Mom gave up arguing with her.

I had just found a nice tan leather jacket that was perfect, except for the price, when a woman's voice rapped out, "Young lady! Get out from there!"

Mom and I both jumped and spun around. Shamefaced and rumpled, Phoebe crawled out from behind a metal cabinet in the corner. The salesclerk who glared at her was short and compact, and her close-trimmed hair was flaming red.

I caught my breath. I could be looking at my own future reflection, the image of myself that might greet me in the mirror twenty years from now.

"I'm sorry," Mom was saying. "Phoebe, get over here! Behave yourself."

Phoebe drooped back over to us, like a puppy with its tail between its legs.

The salesclerk's face softened into a smile. "I know — shopping's a drag," she told Phoebe. My heart lurched as she turned her attention to Mom and me. "May I help you with something?"

I couldn't get a word out. Mom had to do all of the explaining about the type of jacket I wanted, while I stared at that red hair. Any moment now the salesclerk would break off her stream of talk about brand names and sizes, and really *look* at me. Our eyes would meet, and she would know me for who I was . . .

"This is the one you like best, isn't it?" she asked me, swinging the tan jacket from its hanger.

I nodded. "Yeah," I managed. "It's cool."

She did look directly at me when I spoke. I felt her smile all through me. "Try it on again," she said, and when I had slipped into it once more she stepped back for a long, thoughtful look. "Well, I can see why you like it," she said. "I can sympathize — it's tough to find things that go with red hair. That jacket really suits you."

Mom hesitated. Then she dug into her wallet for her charge card. The salesclerk with the red hair escorted us to the checkout counter. "Good choice," she said, winking at me. I waited breathlessly for knowledge to flash between us, for the certainty that would freeze us in the moment where we stood. But she only waved and disappeared among the racks again.

Through the days that followed, I thought I saw my mother everywhere I went. I spied her in passing cars on the Expressway. She looked out at me from magazine ads, extolling facial creams and toothpaste and Caribbean cruises. One night I thought I found her on the five o'clock news, talking about recycling aluminum cans.

But day after day, the call we awaited never came. Dad grew silent and morose. He dragged home a heavier briefcase than usual, and shut himself up in the den with his charts and files. Mom was short-tempered and jumpy, and poor Phoebe bounced nervously from room to room, getting in everyone's way.

Each time the phone rang, we all went taut with hope and dread. Phoebe, who loved carrying important messages, would make a wild dash for the nearest extension. "Whitaker residence," she would chirp, the way Dad had trained her, and her voice would quiver with excitement.

If Dad answered, he spoke slowly, measuring his words so that even "Hello" sounded full of some hidden meaning. Mom's "Hello" was high and quick, brittle with anxiety.

Sometimes I tried to race Phoebe for the phone. But more often I couldn't bring myself to answer at all. My feet took root, and I could only wait and listen as someone else went to pick up the receiver.

The phone rang constantly. Clients called for Dad. Phoebe's friend Emily called to ask her about their homework assignment. The Purple Heart Veterans called, wondering if we had any old clothes to donate. People called to sell us storm windows and lightbulbs and magazine subscriptions. None of them was my mother.

The phone was ringing when I came in the front

door after school Monday afternoon. It would stop before I reached it — but still I dropped my books and rushed into the den. One ring . . . two . . . three . . . "Hello?" I gasped, my chest throbbing.

"Hello, is this Mrs. Whitaker?" It was a woman's voice, cautious, uncertain. It could be — oh, this time it must be . . .

"No. This is her — you know — her daughter."

"Well, may I speak with your mother then?" The voice breezed on, building confidence. "I'm calling from the Piney Knolls Funeral Service."

"You are?" A ghastly thought engulfed me. They weren't telling me the truth. All this talk about a transplant, it was just to keep my spirits up. I was going downhill, falling fast. Already they were thinking of arrangements.

"She's not home," I heard myself explain. "Maybe — try later."

"All right, dear. We're just calling people in your area, talking with them about family cemetery plots. We have a special offer right now at Piney Knolls. It's never too soon to plan for eventualities, you know. But — I'll call your mother back later."

Relief washed over me as I set down the receiver. She had simply pulled our number out of the telephone book. She didn't know anything about me, about kidney failure and the ups and downs of dialysis.

Yet, I wondered, was it truly by accident that

the Piney Knolls Funeral Service had chosen our number? The call had the feel of a message, a message aimed straight at me. I was in perpetual danger. But throughout my illness, no one had ever told me directly that I might die. I had sensed it that first morning when they rushed me to the hospital, but later I had pushed the thought far back into a corner of my mind, back behind all the words about having a positive outlook and sticking to my diet.

Death stalked me every day. My treatments fought it away from me, but the enemy was patient, crouching in wait.

Whoever my mother was, I would be asking her to offer me the gift of life.

# 13

"**P**eanut butter!"

    I whirled from the open door of my locker, nearly jolted off balance by the urgent voice behind me. For a second I didn't recognize the boy who grinned at me from under a crop of blond curls. But only for a second. "Jelly!" I exclaimed, and we both giggled.

"Coming to the meeting?" Chip asked.

"Wow! It's today? I almost forgot."

"You can't forget," he said, sounding hurt. "How could you forget the Secret Society?"

It's easy, I could have told him, when you're waiting for a phone call that will unravel the mystery of your birth and determine your future. Under the circumstances, the Secret Society had a way of dwindling in importance.

It dwindled, but it didn't disappear. After the last bell of the day, I retreated from the mob scrambling for the front door, and made my way up to Miss Perlman's room.

For over an hour, the Secret Society pored through the Last Will and Testament of the eighth-grade class. Forms had been handed out in the fall, but only about half of the kids had bothered to turn them in. We had to make up a lot of legacies. In some cases it was easy. Geri Rabinovich was into horses, and so was one of the seventh-graders. We all agreed on, "I, Geri Rabinovich, leave a year's supply of sugar lumps to Corinne Stevenson."

Other people — those who had no outstanding interest or character trait — were more of a challenge. Larry Shulik was quiet and solemn and bland as tapioca. But Chip remembered that Larry almost always had a wad of gum in his mouth. After arguing and laughing and arguing some more, we ended up with, "I, Larry Shulik, leave a pack of Double-Mint to each of the entering eighth-graders."

Melanie scanned down the rest of the "unaccounted for" list. "Rachel," she said accusingly, "we don't have anything from you."

I hung my head. Before I could concoct an apology, Chip chimed in, "Think it up now. We'll time you. You've got five minutes."

Well, it was only fitting that I should make a will. I was "the bionic girl," kept alive by the miracles of technology. I, Rachel Whitaker, leave my body to Mr. Ciardi, for his collection of specimens in the science room . . .

"No ideas?" Chip teased. "Come on, you can think of something."

"My ballet slippers," I muttered. After all, I probably wouldn't need them again. "I'll leave my ballet slippers to — "

"To Trudy Slesinger," Gloria quipped. Trudy was not only the biggest girl in the seventh grade, but in the entire school. On the playground they called her "Sherman," for "Sherman tank."

Miss Perlman cleared her throat. I guess she felt it her professional duty to keep things from getting out of hand. "I'll leave them to Ms. Lundy," I decided. "She can use them in phys ed class." Not exactly sidesplitting, but it would do.

Suppose that some day my treatment couldn't keep me going. Dr. Wong and Elena admitted that dialysis was tough on the body. I was doing okay now, but how long could that last? Was it morbid to think about dying — or was it realistic?

Maybe I ought to make preparations. Lici should have my ballet things. And my books should go to Phoebe — she read too many computer manuals and not enough good stories. It sounded melodramatic to write a will. But if I died, I wanted my things to go to people who would treasure them. Treasure them, and remember me.

"Hey, Rachel," Chip called. "You're awfully quiet. You still with us?"

"Yeah," I said. "For now."

"If the phone rings in a few minutes, nobody get excited,"Mom announced at dinner. "It's only Karen from work. My program wouldn't run this afternoon."

"Bravo!" Dad exclaimed. "We can lean back and eat in peace."

"When it rings, let's ignore it, just for fun," I said, giggling. "Just to prove we can."

"We can't," Mom said, but she was smiling, too. "I've got to find out if she worked out the bugs for me."

"I got Number Thirty-Six this afternoon," Phoebe broke in. "I mean, speaking of working out bugs. It took me an hour."

"Thirty-six what?" I asked. My hand crept toward my glass of water, but I wouldn't take another sip yet. I'd save it until I finished my macaroni.

"The puzzle," Phoebe said. "You know, the one with all the pieces that fit in different combinations."

"You're still working on that thing?"

"I haven't finished it yet," she said. "I've still got twelve solutions to go."

"That's determination," I remarked. "If that thing had been mine I'd have pitched it in the trash by now."

I swallowed the last bone-dry forkful of noodles, and picked up my glass. An inch of water shimmered at the bottom. I took one sip, then another and another. I was so thirsty I couldn't stop. In a moment it was all gone. The glass was empty.

That little taste only made me long for more. But I had used up my quota. I'd have to last until bedtime. Then I was allowed a quarter of a cup — four tablespoons.

To distract myself, I began clearing the table. Mom scraped the plates, and I rinsed and stacked them in the dishwasher.

"I'll take this garbage out," Mom said. "It's overflowing."

She was already down the back steps with the bulging plastic bag when the phone clamored in the hall. "There it is!" I shouted. "For you!" But the door swung shut, and she couldn't hear me.

The phone jangled again, twice, three times, and nobody moved. Dad sat in the den with the TV on, and Phoebe lay sprawled on the living-room floor doing homework. This call, at least, didn't matter. This once, we were not slaves of the telephone.

My heart wasn't even jumping as I sauntered into the hall and lifted the receiver. Hi, Karen would say in that jaunty, businesslike voice of hers. Hi, your mom around? Just tell her the program ran like a dream . . .

"Hello?" I said. I almost said, "Hello, Karen." But as I spoke, I heard the faint hiss of long-distance wires.

For a moment the line hummed quietly to itself. The call was a mistake. Whoever it was, they were going to hang up without saying anything . . .

"Yes, is this the Whitaker residence?"

I giggled. I was so used to the way Phoebe said "Whitaker residence," so ultraserious in her little-kid voice. It sounded all wrong in the careful, questioning tone of the strange woman on the other end.

"Is this 555-9671?" she asked, her voice rising.

"You have the right number," I said, and waited, my mind closing slowly, firmly, upon certainty.

We were playing a guessing game. It was up to her to ask the next question. I was the one who held the answers.

"Okay then — may I speak to Mrs. Whitaker?"

"She's out right now." What was the matter with me? Mom was forty feet away, rattling open the lid of the garbage pail. But in this crucial moment, I was in control. I would give the answers I chose, and ask some of my own questions.

"Let me take your name and your number," I said, reaching for the scratch pad.

"Well — " The stranger hesitated. Suppose she simply hung up, and never called again? Calmly and deliberately I was destroying my own chances — my chance to get the transplant I needed, my chance to learn the truth.

"My name is Vera Stasic," the voice said. "You

122

want me to spell that? It's S-t-a — "

The back door banged open, and Mom wiped her feet on the rubber mat. "That for me?" she asked.

"Wait a minute," I told Vera Stasic. "She just walked in. Here — you can talk to — " It was my turn to hesitate. What should I call Mom when I was speaking to this woman who must be — who had to be . . . "I'll let you talk to Mrs. Whitaker."

In the next instant, my calm dissolved. I held out the receiver with a trembling hand, and collapsed onto a chair. A wave of heat swept up my whole body, but my hands were icy cold.

Mom glanced at me, puzzled. Then her face went white. "Hello," she said, "this is Linda Whitaker. How can I help you?"

There was a long, long silence. Now and then Mom murmured, "Mm-hmm" or gave a quick, nervous laugh. "Yes," she said once, "we have been — well, a little edgy. Wondering, you know."

A little edgy? What was she talking about? In another twenty-four hours, the house would have exploded!

"Yes . . . yes, I can understand that . . ."

Understand what? I couldn't understand a thing! Everything was out of my hands now. They were talking to each other — my two mothers — and I was expected to sit with my hands on my lap, waiting again.

Suddenly I jumped to my feet. I burst from the kitchen, crossed the dining room in two bounds, and raced up the stairs with energy I had almost forgotten. I paused on the landing at the top, and softly, gingerly, lifted the extension phone.

". . . arrange some time off," Vera Stasic was saying. "Things get pretty complicated at the office."

"Don't I know it," Mom said.

"So I didn't want to call until I could give you something definite. It was all, well, kind of un-expected, if you know what I mean."

"Yes, it must have been," Mom said. She sounded so steady, as if she were talking to Karen after all.

What was the "something definite" Vera Stasic could give us? Had I missed it while I was running upstairs? Or was she still thinking it over? *What* was going on?

"It's a big decision," she was saying. "Not some-thing you can just snap your fingers and say, 'Yeah, I'll do it tomorrow.' So I think what I need to do is come out and meet you and — " her voice dropped almost to a whisper, "you and Rachel."

"We'd like to meet you, too. How soon can you come?" I heard a quaver in Mom's voice. She wasn't as steady as I had thought.

"A week from tomorrow," Vera Stasic said. "That'll be a Friday. How about if we meet some-where Friday night, just kind of touch bases. Then

Saturday, if we want, there'll be more time to talk."

"Why don't you come over here?" Mom suggested. "We can pick you up at the airport."

The details blurred as I listened. I tried to turn the clipped, practical voice on the phone into a picture, but the images all melted together. She was graceful and willowy, with shining black hair; she had broad, imposing shoulders and a heavy frown; she was blonde and shining like a model on a magazine cover, too splendid to bother with people like us.

But she *was* going to bother. She was coming to Chicago, just to meet us.

Mom was giving our address. We could have dessert, she said, dessert and coffee.

"Thanks. That'd be nice," Vera Stasic said. "Well, look, I'll be seeing you next week, then."

"Yes," said Mom. "I'll explain everything to Rachel. She's very anxious — "

"I'm here," I broke in. "On the phone upstairs."

"Oh, Rachel," Mom began, and for a moment I thought she would launch into a lecture about the sin of eavesdropping. But she didn't say anything more.

"Hello, Rachel," Vera Stasic said. She paused, and now I saw her face as flushed, with dark, timid eyes like a deer's. "It was you, who answered the phone."

"Yeah." I couldn't think of anything else to say.

She might be as curious about me as I was about her. No, for me it was beyond curiosity. I was thirsty for knowledge about this woman, thirstier than I ever was for a sip of cold water.

But all she said was, "I'll see you next Friday."

# 14

"**I** see a blue car!" Phoebe bounced up and down on the couch, pointing frantically toward the picture window. "It's stopping! It's stopping!"

For the fourth time in the past half hour, I hurried over to peer outside. A dim figure emerged from the car, and the door slammed. Again I caught my breath. But the figure marched directly up the Ulasovitches' front steps and disappeared.

"False alarm," Phoebe sighed. "How much longer till she gets here?"

"I don't know," I said. "She told Mom her flight comes in from Los Angeles at five-twenty-eight. Then she had to get her luggage and pick up her rental car — I guess it could still take her a while."

"Waiting around is boring," Phoebe said. "I want to see what she looks like."

"You're not the only one!" I flung myself down on the couch. I had prowled through the day like a cat. Sometimes I felt so heavy and lazy I wanted to curl up and sleep, and wake when the excitement was safely behind me. But mostly I was taut and alert, coiled to jump at the slightest sound. Waiting. Waiting . . .

My legs twitched, my hands hungered for something to do. I sprang up again and burst into the kitchen, where Mom had the makings of dessert and coffee on the counter. "I'll put these out," I announced, grabbing a stack of dishes.

"I thought I'd serve the pie out here," Mom called after me, but I barely heard her. I rushed around the table, tossing down a dish at each place, and flew back into the kitchen for something else.

"Rachel, take it easy!" Mom exclaimed. "It's going to be okay!"

"What is?" I had so many worries, I wasn't sure which one Mom meant to allay. It would be okay — my birth mother would land on schedule and find the house without getting lost? It would be okay — she'd be sweet and lovely, not a horror, no one to be afraid of? It would be just fine — she would graciously offer me a kidney?

I picked up the pie. It was lemon meringue, the top covered with delicious-looking mounds and swirls. In honor of the occasion, Mom had bought it special at the fanciest bakery in the neighborhood, and I could have a little slice myself. I headed for the dining-room table again.

I'll never know how it happened. Suddenly, as if some gremlin reached out and grabbed me, the toe of my shoe caught on something invisible. I was on the floor before I realized I was falling. The pie spun out of my hands and alighted, pan-side up, on the carpet in front of me.

At that very moment, the doorbell rang.

"Wait!" Mom cried. "I'll get that — no, I'll go to the door, you — " She trailed into confusion, gazing down at the mess. Then, like somebody in a movie, she covered her eyes with her hands. I opened my mouth to cry, but a burst of laughter came out instead.

I was still giggling helplessly as we flocked to the front door — Mom and Phoebe and me, and Dad bringing up the rear. For a second we all stood there, immobilized. Then I heard a footstep on the porch, and a woman clearing her throat. The bell rang again.

I stepped forward and pulled the door open. She stood in the glow of the porch light, a petite figure with an embroidered cloth bag swinging from one shoulder. From beneath her paisley scarf peeked a wisp of carrot-red hair.

"Hi," I gasped, staggering back. I couldn't find any more words.

Fortunately, Mom was right there to take over. "Come on in!" she exclaimed, holding out her hand. "You must be worn out. That's a long flight, isn't it?"

She was here — Vera Stasic — in our living room, smiling and nodding through the introductions. Through the pounding in my ears I heard Mom saying, "I'm Linda Whitaker . . . and this is my husband, Tom . . . and Phoebe . . . and — "

Vera Stasic looked straight at me and held out her hand. "And Rachel," she said, so softly it was almost a whisper. Her fingers were cold and quick, brushing mine. I drew back hastily to watch her from a little distance. I still had nothing to say.

"Was your plane on time?" Dad asked. He and Vera launched into a discussion of O'Hare Airport. They seemed to agree that congestion was the big problem. Too many flights in and out, not enough space, planes stalled on the runways . . . It was the sort of conversation Dad might have with a client — courteous, cool, and businesslike. But this wasn't some stranger who wanted to buy insurance. It was Vera Stasic. It was my mother.

"Let me take your things," Mom said. Smoothly, gracefully, Vera Stasic slipped out of the jacket and unwound the scarf. Her red hair tumbled around her shoulders. "I forget what houses are like back east," she said. "Built to hold in the heat. In California, everything is so much more open, airy — lots of flowers, even at this time of year."

"Our crocuses are popping up," Phoebe chimed in, as though she had to defend Chicago.

"Yes," Mom added, "we do have spring here, sort of."

We all looked at one another through a painful silence. I was dizzy. My heart galloped, I could barely breathe. I couldn't stop staring, but I couldn't quite believe that I was really seeing her.

She was pretty. She looked crisp and cool in her tailored blue suit, as though she had just stepped out of her own front door and had everything under control. She was quick, efficient, utterly sophisticated.

So my mother was not a bag lady, not a nurse or a salesclerk in girls' jackets. I would never again glimpse her by surprise in a crowd on the lakefront or running up an escalator at Sears. There was no penthouse in Manhattan, no farmhouse with a weather vane.

For almost as long as I could remember, I had secretly played the Mother Game. I had pretended a thousand stories, and always there were still more people my mother might be. Since the search began, the game had gathered power, had filled up a place in the center of my life. And now it was over. I had never guessed that it would hurt so much to say good-bye to all those possibilities, to the dazzling ones and even to the ones that appalled me.

Now the mystery was gone. I was left with one woman, a being of flesh and blood. The name and the voice had three dimensions.

"If you like, we have some nice — " Mom began. Then her face went blank for a moment, and we both remembered the pie again. "We have — well, we have a minor disaster," she finished, and mustered a ragged laugh.

Vera Stasic glanced in the direction we were all looking. Nothing had changed. The pie lay face down, telltale rivulets of lemon filling squeezing out from under the rim of the pan.

Vera Stasic looked like someone who never tripped, who never dropped so much as a nickel. "Yes, I see what you mean," she said. "If you've got a spatula — or a big sheet of cardboard maybe — "

"It was my fault," I blurted. "I fell. I never used to be such a klutz, before I got sick."

Instantly I wished I could bite back the words. It sounded like such a bid for sympathy! I hadn't meant to pressure her. I would never come straight out and ask her to donate a kidney — it was unthinkable! I wasn't sure I wanted anything from her at all — certainly not some hidden, vital part of her body. The very thought made me writhe inside with embarrassment, revulsion. It would tie me to her, this polite stranger, forever.

But I was tied to her already. She had brought me into the world in the first place. We shared a common set of ancestors. She could tell me about aunts, cousins, grandparents I had never known. Our red hair was only the beginning.

Somehow the pie got scraped off the carpet, and Mom unearthed a package of Oreos. We all took our places at the dining-room table. After the milk and sugar made their rounds, and I poured a splash of Coke into my glass, silence threatened.

Vera Stasic was watching me. Whenever I looked her way, her gaze met mine. "Aren't you having anything more to drink?" she asked.

"I can't," I said. "I mean, I'm not supposed to have too much liquid."

"Oh. I didn't know that." She shifted uneasily on her chair. I couldn't think of anything to say that would make her more comfortable.

"What sort of work did you say you do in California?" Mom asked hastily.

"I probably didn't. I'm with a company that makes educational toys, things they use in the schools. I'm the head of product development."

Right away, Phoebe's interest perked up. "What kind of toys?" she wanted to know. "Did you bring some with you?"

Vera Stasic shook her head. "I guess I thought," she cast me a sidelong glance, "I thought, thirteen, that's too old. It never occurred to me Rachel might have a little sister."

"That's okay," Phoebe assured her. "I'm probably too old, too. I'm in third grade." She paused and added, "What kind of toys are they?"

"Well, we have games to teach the alphabet, blocks with letters and pictures and all that. And number games. And we've got a lot of gadgets for teaching science."

That was all Phoebe needed. The next thing I knew, she had a pencil and a pad of paper, and they were bending over her plans for a contraption with balls to represent the solar system. You sat on a bicycle seat and worked a set of pedals to make the planets revolve.

For the next few minutes Vera Stasic stopped watching me, and I was free to study her in peace. But soon, to my own annoyance, I felt a twinge of jealousy. *I* was her daughter. And here she was chatting away with Phoebe about some stupid game! Maybe Vera Stasic thought I was boring — besides being so clumsy I couldn't carry a lemon meringue pie. Maybe she wished that Phoebe was really her child.

After a while Mom and I got up and cleared the table. I was rinsing cups at the sink when Vera Stasic came in and stood right beside me. "This is all so strange," she said in a rush. "I still can't quite take it in."

Mom shut the dishwasher and straightened up. "It is for us, too," she said. "It's hard to know how to begin. How to talk about — about the reason you're here."

"You've all been through a lot, I guess," Vera Stasic said. "And now I'm stretching it out even more. You need an answer, something definite from me."

Mom nodded. I stood still, hardly breathing.

"I think what I need to do," Vera Stasic went on, "I need to have a little time with Rachel alone."

At the sound of my name, I jumped as though a firecracker had exploded outside the window. She *did* want to know me, then. But the thought of it, just the two of us off somewhere by ourselves, filled me with panic. I wouldn't be able to speak. I would burn with questions, with things I needed to say to her while I had this one chance, and I wouldn't be able to get any words out. I was so slow and heavy, puffy and dried-out — I was sure to disappoint her.

"I have to get back to my hotel," she was saying. "Rachel, are you free any time tomorrow?"

I swallowed hard. "Any time," I said. "Whenever you want."

"How about I stop by around nine," she said. "We can go out somewhere, walk around, just talk for a while. All right with you?"

"Sure," I said. "It's fine."

For one heartbeat I thought she was going to pat my shoulder, the way Mom would if she were sending me off to school for a big exam. But she pulled back her hand just in time. "Well, I'd better be going," she said. "I've got to make some phone calls."

Trailing good-byes, she headed for the front door. Suddenly Mom burst out, "I see it now! I really see it!"

"What?" Vera Stasic asked, bewildered.

"It's the way you lift your shoulders," Mom said. "Like you're setting out, taking on the world — very determined. It's Rachel's gesture. Unmistakable."

The three of us gazed at each other in wonder, locked together in the moment of recognition. It was true, then. Standing there in the vestibule, near enough to touch, we were three points of a triangle — me, and the two women who were each my mother.

# 15

"You know, this is my first visit to Chicago. Think you can show me around?"

I nodded doubtfully, snapping my seatbelt. The inside of the rented car smelled new. Classical music poured from the radio, the rich, powerful chords of a piano sonata. Vera Stasic's hands on the wheel were slender and delicate, with long, polished nails. On one finger a diamond ring sparkled.

"What do you want me to call you?" I asked abruptly.

I was a little afraid she would want me to call her Mother, but instead she asked, "What would you like to call me?"

"Well . . . I keep thinking of you as Vera Stasic."

"How about just plain Vera? Would that be okay?"

"Yes," I said, relieved. "That'll be fine."

It was one of those unexpected days in March when winter suddenly melts away, and the world celebrates the coming of spring. On the pavement, people hurried along in shirt sleeves, and every face I saw seemed to be smiling. It would be a great day for walking. "We can go downtown, to State Street and Grant Park, and — there are lots of neat places down there."

"Point the way," Vera said. "Wherever you say, we'll go."

I felt like an old-time Chicagoan, directing her on and off the Expressway, and showing her through the crowded streets of the Loop. I was just about to warn her that you can never find parking downtown, when we pulled into an empty place, right in the middle of everything. I had a feeling it was going to be that kind of day.

"What should we see?" Vera asked. "What do you recommend?"

This was no casual tour of the Windy City. It was a test, an assessment of my character. I heard every word I uttered as it must sound in Vera's ears. I squirmed when I thought of what she saw each time she looked at me. Even if I possessed my old energy, I would still seem dull and dumpy by her standards. She was so sophisticated, manicured, balanced. Beside her, I had never felt more ordinary in my life.

"If we walk up this way, you can go to Marshall Field's," I said, eying her elegant purple pants suit and suede jacket. "I think it's about the fanciest store in the world."

Her eyes lit up as we swished through the revolving doors. Marshall Field's is not just expensive, it's high-class. Our feet sank soundlessly into thick carpeting as we cruised the broad, uncluttered aisles. In that atmosphere of hushed elegance, we kept our voices low. I could tell that Vera was enthralled as we wandered through displays of streamlined modern furniture, cast-iron cookware, stately grandfather clocks. Slowly, I began to relax. At least I had scored a success this time. But the day still stretched ahead of me, endless and unpredictable.

In the appliance department, Vera stopped short before a wide-screen television set, built into an elaborately carved walnut cabinet. "They've got to be kidding!" she exclaimed, and her voice soared through the still, tranquil air like a siren. "Look at the price on this thing!"

Astonished, I glanced from her to the price card that rested discreetly atop the cabinet. I had to read it twice, to make sure I hadn't imagined an extra couple of zeros.

"Ten thousand dollars!" I cried. "For a *TV*?"

"It ought to have solid gold knobs," Vera said. "And a genie who pops out to turn it on for you."

Suddenly we were both laughing, wildly, out of control. A well-dressed elderly couple turned and frowned at us, and a salesclerk shook his head disapprovingly, but neither of us could stop. "We'd better get out of here, before they throw us out!" Vera said, and we scrambled for the escalator.

"You'd have to build a special room for it," I said, as we coasted downward. "Maybe charge admission."

"Admission just to look at it, not to watch it," Vera added. "If they want to watch a program, they have to submit personal references first."

The revolving doors swished again, and we stood in the sun, still quivering with the last delicious giggles. Laughing transformed Vera. She was still chic, but her careful, businesslike veneer had cracked. Her eyes danced with mischief. "It's almost sacrilegious, to raise your voice in there," she said, grinning. "Like dropping the collection plate in church."

"Did you ever do that?" I asked.

"When I was about twelve," she said. "I was sitting there in Mass, really bored, and they passed the plate down our pew — and I was just fooling around. I made a really fierce grab for it, pretending like it was a holdup to make my sister laugh — and somehow I tipped the thing too far and there was money jingling all over the floor!"

"What happened to you? Did you get in trouble?"

"My father was mad," she said. "He had quite a temper. But he couldn't hit me right there in front of everybody. By the time we got out, he'd cooled down."

"Your father," I repeated. "That was my grandfather."

We began to walk, but I didn't notice where we were going. I only wanted to listen to her tell stories of her life, of all the people who were my blood kin. "He had a temper all right." Vera sighed. "About three years ago he was watching the Red Sox, got so mad at one of the calls he had a heart attack and died on the spot."

"Oh no!" It didn't seem fair — that this grandfather of mine was already gone, before I would ever know him. "Is your mother still alive?" I asked anxiously. "And you said you have a sister, right?"

"Oh, my mother's very much alive," Vera said with a wry smile. "Trying to run the whole world. My sister Mary, the one I was showing off for that time in church, she's married with three kids. Then I've got another sister and two brothers. Five of us altogether."

"Wow!" I said. "It must have been fun, growing up in such a big family."

For a few seconds Vera was quiet. "Well, it had some nice moments," she said at last. "But mostly, there wasn't enough of anything to go around. Not enough clothes, not enough servings at meals. Not enough time for Mom to help us with homework. I guess we were economically deprived. We just called it good old-fashioned poor."

"But you didn't stay poor," I said. Judging by

her wardrobe, that was an understatement.

"No," she agreed, but she didn't smile. "I made it out of there."

We had reached Michigan Avenue, with its glass and steel towers. Across the street Grant Park beckoned like a green oasis. "Can we go over there for a while?" I asked. In a flash I saw myself as a little kid, tugging at my mother's hand —and the mother in the picture was not Mom, but Vera.

"We think alike," she said. And as we crossed over, she took my hand.

At first we just wandered. The park was alive with people bursting from their winter hibernation. Joggers pounded up and down the paths, dodging speeders on bicycles. We paused to listen to a boy in a University of Illinois T-shirt, who played a wailing jazz saxophone. Soon he was the center of a small, admiring crowd. "Are we supposed to give him some money?" Vera wondered. But he had no tin cup. He just played for sheer pleasure.

I was starting to feel tired, and wishing I could sit down without bringing on a parade of questions about my health, when Vera announced, "We don't walk like this in California. If we go two blocks to the mailbox, we jump in the car."

"We could sit on one of those benches," I said, still playing tour guide. "That's Buckingham Fountain over there. It's turned on in the summer, and it goes off every hour like Old Faithful."

"This is really quite nice," Vera said as we settled down. "When I first found out you were growing up in Chicago, I thought, oh, no! That poor kid! What have they done to her!"

"You did?" For the first time she had touched upon the choice she had made more than thirteen years ago.

"Well, Chicago — it makes you think of Al Capone, gangs, dirty politics. But then I thought, it had to be better than Bridgeport. That's where you'd have grown up if you lived with me."

"Bridgeport?" I said numbly. This was no time to get sidetracked into a geography lesson. I wanted to talk about my beginnings, no matter where they were. "That wasn't the only reason," I blurted out. "You didn't put me up for adoption just so I might live in a different city."

"No." Vera turned away, gazing across the grass. A little boy dashed by with a fluttering kite, but she wasn't looking at him. She was somewhere else, unreachably remote.

After a minute she turned back, but she didn't quite look at me as she began, "Bridgeport was part of it. I wanted you to escape. I pictured you growing up in a pretty little house with a white picket fence, and a cat and a dog and summers in the country. I remember looking through the glass in the nursery and telling myself you would have a pool in your backyard, and swim like a fish by the time you were three."

"We never had a pool," I said. "I learned at the Y."

Vera faced me now, her smile tentative, almost shy. "I was convinced I was doing it for your own good. That's what my mother told me. And the social worker in the hospital. And my best friend at work. Everybody said, 'You're in no position to take care of a baby. Put it up for adoption, it will be better off.' "

"How old were you?" I asked. She hadn't been thirteen, anyway — not if she was already working.

"I was almost twenty. I had a good job — I was a secretary in an office. You had to look nice, get dressed up every day, have your hair done. Everybody else I knew worked in a factory, if they worked at all. So I was hiking up the ladder."

"And then you had me."

"I was going as far and as fast as it was humanly possible to travel. Nothing was going to stop me." She was quiet for a moment, before she added in a low, aching voice, "Not even you."

Suddenly, I blazed with anger. All that talk about wanting me to escape — she'd been lying to herself, lying to me. She just couldn't be weighed down by an unwanted kid. She hadn't been willing to sacrifice her precious plans to make room in her life for me. It had been easier to hand me over to strangers.

Still, she hadn't told me the entire story. I needed to hear it all. "Who was my birth father?" I asked.

"His name was David Harkness," Vera said.

I searched for a tinge of yearning in her voice. Her cheeks didn't even flush when she mentioned him. Maybe he was a real bum, a disastrous mistake she wanted to forget. And he was part of me, just as much as she was.

"What was he like?" I asked. Somehow I automatically put him in the past tense.

"Charming, and smart. And he'd been to college. I think that was the part that really impressed me. He worked for the same company I did. We were going to get married. I thought I was in love with him, but I guess really I saw him as my ticket. He was going to take me where I wanted to get to."

"But he didn't?" I prodded.

She shook her head with a wry laugh. "The furthest he ever took me was New Haven," she said. "One night we had dinner at this fancy restaurant. The Yale students went there when their parents were in town. The next day I told him you were on the way — and three weeks later he had a job transfer to Cincinnati."

"Just like that, you never saw him again?"

Vera's thumb and forefinger snipped the air. "Like that. Gone. Unlisted phone. Letters came back, 'Addressee Unknown.' I think he quit his job out there, or got fired. I still don't know for sure."

Vera wasn't to blame after all — it was this David Harkness, my charming, smart father. "He sounds like a jerk," I said.

"Oh, he wasn't such a bad guy," she assured me. "He was just too young. He needed another five or six years to grow up and get his head on straight."

"So you were all alone then, after he left," I said, awed. She talked about it calmly now, but it must have been unbearable. I remembered how awful I felt when I realized that Danny Kuczinski didn't like me and never would — and I hadn't been planning to marry him, with a baby on the way.

"My dad was ready to kill me," she said. "But my mom was pretty cool about it all, and my sister Mary was terrific. I never went into one of those places for unwed mothers. I just stayed home until you were born."

"Did they ever tell you about the family that adopted me?" I wondered aloud.

"The social workers wouldn't say much. Just that your father was in insurance — like half the people in Connecticut."

"They wouldn't even give you pictures? I would think you'd want to see what kind of people they were."

"I wanted something. I'm not sure what it was, but I didn't get it. Not till now."

I wasn't angry at anyone anymore. I felt as though my whole body were washed with warm, gentle light.

"Funny, how I should find you just now," she mused. "My life is coming together in every other way. I love my job, and I'm getting married in August. The only missing piece was knowing you were all right."

"You're getting married?" I exclaimed.

She held out her hand, and her ring caught the sunlight. "His name is Brent," she said, digging into her purse. "Here. I took this a couple of weeks ago."

"He looks nice," I said, studying the photograph. "I like his smile."

"He *is* nice," Vera said. "I'm very, very lucky."

We were quiet for a while, wandering into our separate thoughts. At last Vera broke the silence. "Tell me about yourself," she said. "Who are your friends? What's your favorite subject? What do you like to do?"

"I like reading and I hate math. My best friend is Lici Flores."

"What else? Tell me anything. What's your life like?"

"Oh . . . it's hard to know where to start." I had to choose my words carefully, to fit as much as I could into the little bit of time we had. "I'm pretty good at drawing," I told her. "I've been doing it a lot more this year, and I really do like it. But the thing I love most of all is ballet."

"Ballet?" I read a tangle of emotions in Vera's face — amazement, disbelief, delight. "*I* was into ballet for about four years — really into it! Wow! This is incredible!"

My questions flooded out all at once. "What kind of ballet did you study? When did you start? Why didn't you stay with it? Did you have the same teacher the whole time, or did you switch around?"

"I started when I was nine," Vera said. "There was a community center by our house, and they had classes for the kids in the neighborhood. The teacher gave me a lot of encouragement, really wanted me to stick with it. But then when I was thirteen I broke my ankle doing a leap, and by the time it healed, the center had cut back and ballet was a casualty. My parents didn't have the money to send me to an expensive class somewhere. So that was the end of it."

"But how did you stand it?" I asked. "Didn't you always feel like something was missing? I don't think I'll ever get used to it."

"You mean, you stopped dancing? Why?"

I stared down at my hands, knotted together on my lap. "I just couldn't do it very well anymore. After I went on dialysis."

Vera touched my shoulder. Leaping beyond

words, her touch spoke her sorrow, and her understanding. "Even if it's different now, even if it's harder — don't give up," she said. "Do the best that you can."

Tears stung my eyes. I could barely speak. "It wouldn't be good enough. I don't belong there anymore."

"Maybe you'll feel better about it if you have a transplant. I'm going in for the blood work on Monday."

"A transplant?" I repeated. Somehow, in the tumult of the last twenty-four hours, I had nearly put it out of my mind. "You want to go ahead with it then?"

"I must have made up my mind the day the social worker called me. I just didn't know it. I kept reminding myself what a big decision it was, telling myself I shouldn't rush into anything. But there wasn't any decision. There's only one right thing to do."

"But what if something happens to you?" I cried. "It's not fair — I can't let you take any chances just for me."

"I talked to my doctor. She says it's a very safe procedure. The only thing now is something they call tissue typing. They have to do a lot of blood tests, to make sure we're a good match."

The little boy with the kite raced toward us. It was aloft now, sailing high and steady with its colored tail trailing in the wind.

We were quiet for a little, just watching the crowds of people. At last Vera said, "I guess I'd better be getting you home."

"I suppose so." Slowly we made our way back across the grass. We were quiet on the long walk back to the car. I had learned so much, I needed time to sort through it all, to take it in.

Vera was searching for the car keys when another question darted into my head. It was out before I had a chance to think. "Hey! Can you roll your tongue?"

# 16

"**I** knew we'd be a good match," Vera said, "the second I saw that hair of yours."

"I figured it would work as soon as I found out you were another non-tongue roller." It wasn't easy to keep the mood light, standing in line at hospital admitting, but we were trying hard. Mom and Dad alternated between worry and a sort of festive hilarity, as though we were all setting out on a trip to the beach. Vera was winning them over.

At first, when Vera told them that she intended to donate a kidney to me if the doctors approved, they were grateful. But they were cautious beneath their gratitude, not quite sure they liked her or trusted her completely. Now, though, as we all made our way through the paperwork together, smiles flashed back and forth. My parents surrounded me with their caring and their hope. My father and both of my mothers.

Three months had passed since Vera's first visit to Chicago. After the doctors declared her a "compatible donor," they still had to schedule the surgery. It took forever to get two operating rooms at the same time on a day when the whole surgical team was available. But now Vera was back. The waiting was over at last.

All through those endless months, as spring turned into summer, Vera was on my mind. I thought of how different my life would have been if I had grown up with her. We would have formed our own little universe, just the two of us against the world. I pictured us waving good-bye to the smokestacks of Bridgeport from our car windows, and singing with the radio as we headed across the plains. California — the name was warm and shining as a promise. Vera and I would have shared the discovery of Yosemite, of orange groves and cable cars and beaches.

Compared to Vera, Mom and Dad and even Phoebe seemed to plod from day to day, loaded down with their charts and graphs and computer programs. They had never struggled to survive, fought for success against crushing odds. Experiences like that had to be character-building — and Vera had character.

"She's incredible!" I told Lici, when she came over one afternoon. "You'd really love her."

"Why?" Lici asked. "What makes you think so?"

"She's gorgeous, for one thing. A real sharp

dresser. And she's got a very important job. She has — style."

"Well — " Lici hesitated. She looked over at the aquarium, as if the fish would give her an answer. "You haven't exactly had time to get to know her yet. Maybe you shouldn't be too sure."

"I don't get it!" I exclaimed. "You used to make up stories about who my birth mother might be. Some really wild ones, remember? And now you're telling me to cool it?"

"I just mean — take it easy, Rachel, that's all."

"You wouldn't say that if you met her," I insisted. But Lici shook her head and went on watching the angelfish.

It's hard to take it easy, when your feelings are all tangled together the way mine were. Kathy Wheeling was right about one thing, I discovered after I met Vera. Just the promise of a transplant filled me with a new sense of responsibility and purpose. I longed to show Vera that I deserved her caring. I decided to reenroll in ballet class.

It was a scary moment, walking up to Miss Panova in the studio one afternoon. I half expected her to refuse when I asked to come back. Instead, a smile broke across her face. "You must be feeling better," she said. "Of course you can come back. Can you start Monday?"

I had to set her straight. "I'm about the same, really. It's just — I'm getting out of shape. And I miss dancing so much."

"You can pace yourself," Miss Panova said. "Do whatever you can, that's what's important."

My first day back, I wondered if she regretted her decision. Tight with disuse, my body balked at movements that were once as natural as breathing. But strangely I didn't care. I would bring it back somehow. I would dance again.

"Room 1504," the woman behind the desk told us, stamping the last form. "Check in at the nursing station when you go up. Elevator's on your left."

"It'll be like a slumber party," Vera said, grinning over at me. "We can stay up till midnight telling ghost stories."

"Don't forget, surgery is at eight tomorrow, and they like to get you up hours ahead of time," Mom warned. She could be so literal, squeezing all the fun out of life.

But once we got upstairs, the fun vanished without any help from anybody. "It's that same hospital smell," Mom said, putting my thoughts into words as we walked down the corridor. That heavy blend of medicines and disinfectants swept me back to the tests and the terrors of last fall. I was back — back to that morning when I woke up knowing that my life could slip away from me.

I shivered in my ugly hospital gown. Maybe this was all a mistake. Transplants didn't always work. Suppose my body rejected Vera's kidney. It had betrayed me before, it was capable of anything. I'd be back where I started. And if anything ever happened to Vera's remaining kidney, she would wind up on dialysis herself. What right did I have to let her take that risk?

I was doing all right without a transplant, anyway. I was dancing again, and drawing, too. I had even made some new friends — Melanie and Gloria and Chip from the yearbook staff. I was learning to skip bananas and chocolate, to take the tired days as they came. Dialysis wasn't quite as routine as brushing my teeth, but it no longer loomed at the center of my life.

Did I really want to go through the pain and misery of a major operation, when it might only bring disappointment in the end?

I sat on the bed and let Mom bustle about, unpacking my things. She seemed so anxious to do things for me, I couldn't tell her to stop.

Vera strode out to the nursing station in her floppy paper slippers and came back with a brimming pitcher of ice water. Even in her hospital gown, she clung to a trace of elegance.

"Don't you mind being here?" I demanded. "Don't you wish you were any place else?"

Vera sat on the edge of her bed and opened a jar of nail polish remover. "I'd take this place over Bridgeport," she said.

We were all laughing when the nurse came in with a glass on a tray. She glanced at the ID bracelet on my wrist, to make sure I was the person she had in mind, before she announced, "I've got something for you. This is cyclosporine." She sounded as if she were making introductions at a party.

"Cyclosporine," I repeated. I looked doubtfully at the plastic glass. It was half filled with a murky, orange liquid.

"It's an anti-immune medication," the nurse explained. "It's to keep your body from rejecting your transplant."

"Oh, yeah," I said. "Doctor Wong explained about that." I picked up the glass and sniffed. "It smells like orange juice."

"That's what we mix it with," the nurse said. "Drink it down now."

"Orange juice," I repeated in awe. For months, orange juice had been a forbidden delicacy. And here was a nurse, ordering me to drink it!

"This is just the beginning," the nurse assured me, smiling. "After your transplant, you can have lots of no-nos."

When Mom was sure I had swallowed the last drop, she turned to Vera. "You know," she said awkwardly, "I'm not certain we've said this in quite the right words yet — but we — Rachel's dad and I — we really appreciate what you're doing for us."

Vera looked down at her hands, embarrassed. She didn't answer.

"Are you sure you want to?" I burst out. "You can still change your mind."

"Never," she said simply. "It — it makes everything complete for me somehow. It's hard to explain. I guess after I gave my baby up, there was always something missing in my life. I tried not to think about it much, but it was there. And now — doing this — I'm connected in a way I wasn't before. It's important. It's what I need to do and — " she looked hard at Mom — "I'm glad you've given me this chance to do it."

The next day comes back to me in scraps. I remember two orderlies discussing the Cubs as Vera and I waited for the elevator, side by side on twin stretchers. I know that some time later, through a drugged haze, I asked someone in a white coat — was it one of the surgeons? — whether Vera would be all right. "We haven't lost a donor yet," he said cheerfully. But my foggy brain answered, there's always a first time.

Then I lay on a high, narrow table, and a soothing voice said, "Count backward from a hundred. Come on now. One hundred . . . ninety-nine . . ."

"Ninety-eight," I said obediently. "Ninety-seven." Something pricked my arm, and the room, the voices, even the numbers were gone.

"Rachel, can you hear me?"

I tried to lift my head, but it was too heavy. I

seemed to be tied to a bed, but I couldn't guess where I was. Counting. I was supposed to be counting.

"I lost track," I mumbled. "Where was I? Ninety-seven, ninety-six — "

"You're in Recovery," the voice said. "Your surgery is over. Everything went fine."

Dim and far away, my body throbbed with pain. It came from everywhere at once. My head was being squeezed in a vise. My hand felt big and fiery. A thousand razor blades whirled in my stomach. I hung suspended, somewhere above all that misery. But second by second it was dragging me closer.

"I want — " I began, and stopped. What would help? Would anything take the pain away?

They had cut Vera, too. I wondered if she lay somewhere nearby, hurting just as much as I was.

But I couldn't keep my thoughts on anyone else, not even Vera. "I want," I tried again. "I want my mother!" The mother who had always been there, as long as I could remember, turning on the light to scare away the nightmares. There was no doubt in my mind which mother I needed now.

"She'll be right in. Your mom and dad are both waiting outside."

In less than a moment they leaned above me. "How are you, hon?" Mom asked. Dad just said, "Rachel." Their faces were pale and tired — but they were so familiar, so dear, they pushed the pain a little farther away from me.

Vera and I were in separate rooms now, and I didn't see her until the next afternoon. She padded in, wheeling an IV pole beside her, just in time to catch me with my gown rumpled up past my hips as a nurse gently lifted me off the bedpan. At any other time, I would have been mortified. Instead, it was a moment of pure exhilaration. And Vera was there to share the triumph.

"It works!" I greeted her. "I can hardly believe it! I can pee!"

"Hurray!" Vera cried. "Bravo! *Olé!*"

"I'm like Buckingham Fountain!" I giggled. "Remember, it was turned off all winter? And now — " An aide came in, with juice on a tray. She looked at me with raised eyebrows. But when you haven't been able to pee for close to a year, you don't really care how many strangers give you funny looks. "And now," I went on, "they turned it back on. I'm a miracle of modern science!"

When we were alone, I sank back against the pillows. They had explained to us that Vera would recover more rapidly from her "procedure" than I would from mine. But I could hardly believe that she was already up and walking. My body was still battered and exhausted, and painkillers clouded my mind. But through it all beamed an extraordinary sense of wholeness, of well-being. I was clean. That heavy, polluted feeling was already a fading memory.

Dr. Wong said I might be home in two weeks, and I could go straight back to school. I could buy a large Coke at the cafeteria whenever I wanted. And I could clean out the cupboard in the kitchen, pitch every box of spaghetti into the trash.

None of it would have been possible without Vera.

I smiled over at her, where she sat on one of the straight-backed visitors' chairs. Her hair was combed neatly, but she hadn't put on her makeup today. The hospital was starting to get to her.

I owed her so much! I could never begin to tell her what her gift meant to me. I could only say what I had said before, what I would be saying to her for the rest of my life: "Thank you! Thank you!"

# 17

Taking cyclosporine and my other medicines
was a bit of a hassle sometimes, but I didn't
mind. I felt stronger and healthier every day. The
hospital routine was stifling, and I couldn't wait
to get home. But at the same time, I wanted to
hang onto each day that I could spend there, talking to Vera.

Usually I found her in the solarium, the little
room at the end of the hall where you could read
or watch TV or talk to visitors once you were well
enough to get out of bed. She would be leafing
through a magazine, or writing a letter to Brent.
But she would break into a smile when she saw
me in the doorway, and I would settle beside her
on the couch to ask questions and tell stories.
There were so many questions to ask, so many
stories to tell!

I heard about Vera's sisters and brothers — my
aunts and uncles. Rose's life had always been a
struggle. Sometimes she had a job, and sometimes

she didn't, and she was always falling for men with what Vera called "tragic flaws." Mary was different. She never had much money, but she kept her family going somehow. She had three kids — and Vera showed me their pictures. The oldest girl was eleven, and something about her face told me we would like each other if we ever met. She was my own cousin, after all.

I got Mom to bring in some of our family albums. Vera studied each page, and wanted to know details about every picture. I told her about Miss Elsworth, my first ballet teacher back in Connecticut, and about Miss Panova, and Lici, and my whole class here in Chicago. I showed her a stack of my drawings, and she laughed when I did a caricature of Dr. Wong.

"I can sure tell you two are sisters," a new nurse remarked one morning. "Two peas in a pod."

I opened my mouth to explain, but it seemed too complicated. Besides, I *did* feel a little like Vera was my sister. It fit, somehow.

One afternoon Mom dropped over to see me, and found us engrossed in a game of Scrabble. When I glanced up she was watching us, frowning and silent. Her anxious, troubled face twisted my stomach into knots. "Hi, Mom!" I said, forcing myself to sound cheerful. "I just got *fake* on a triple word — that's thirty-three points!"

"Great," Mom said limply. "I'll meet you down at your room when you get through, okay?" She watched us for a minute or two more, and then she disappeared.

I couldn't concentrate on the game after that. I kept thinking of that look on Mom's face. Suddenly, with a jolt, I knew what was bothering her. It didn't make sense — but she was jealous. Jealous of Vera.

She was waiting in my room when I came in, herself again. She told me Lici had called, wondering if I'd really be home on Monday. She thought Lici was planning some kind of surprise for me, and we tried to guess what it might be.

At last there was a long pause, and Mom's mood shifted again. "You know," she said, "Vera's scheduled to leave in two days."

"Yeah." I looked down at the floor. I hated the thought of losing her, when I had only just found her.

"I hope," Mom said carefully, "I hope you aren't getting — too attached to her."

"What do you mean, 'too attached'?" I flared. "I ought to be attached to her. After everything she's done for me, plus the fact she's my — "

"Yes, I know all that," Mom interrupted. "But she has her own life to go back to. And so do you."

"What's that got to do with anything? We'll keep in touch. Maybe I'll go out and see her sometime. And she can come to Chicago. She travels a lot for her job."

"Well," Mom said, with a chill in her voice, "I

163

don't think she'll be sitting down with us on Thanksgiving."

I flinched as if she had hit me. "What have you got against her?" I demanded.

"I'm sorry," Mom said. "I don't want to sound — mean. I've got nothing against her, believe me — nothing in the world. I just want you to be realistic. I don't want to see you get hurt now, after everything you've already been through."

"Don't worry," I assured her. That wasn't enough. Awkwardly I added, "She won't take me away or anything. I'm still your daughter."

I said good-bye to Vera on Thursday afternoon. I kept trying to smile, but I knew that I'd start to cry if I gave her a hug.

Vera put her hands on my shoulders and looked at me for a long moment, as though she wanted to commit me to memory. "I'm so glad," she said. "Glad I met you, glad I could help. I'm just glad that you're you."

She turned away quickly and picked up her purse. "I might be out here again in October," she said. "Maybe we'll get together then."

"Oh, yes!" I said. "Let's!" But October was nearly four months away. I wondered how I could wait that long to see her again.

When Lici planned a homecoming celebration, she didn't go halfway. Clusters of balloons greeted me from the porch railings, dancing bubbles of red, blue, orange, and yellow. A giant sign proclaimed WELCOME HOME, RACHEL from the trunk of the maple tree. Best of all, Lici herself waved from the front steps. Crowded beside her were Sarah and Tina and Joy, Gloria, Melanie, and Phoebe.

Everybody talked at once as I clambered out of the car. Lici was telling me how she thought I was coming at three o'clock, and had to run frantically to get everything ready when she found out I'd arrive at noon. Melanie said Chip wanted to come, but chickened out when he learned he'd be the only boy.

I was still moving a little slowly. I had lots of warnings from the doctors about not "overdoing" things for a while after surgery. But being with them all again made me want to pirouette.

Gradually the commotion died down and we trooped into the house. On the dining-room table stood a magnificent cake with lavish swirls of chocolate frosting.

"Hey," I said, "I don't know if I'm ready for this yet. Maybe I'd better put a gob of rice on top, just to remind me I'm allowed to eat it."

"It's like you're back from a war zone or something," Phoebe said, sneaking a pinch of icing. "Like, did you win any medals?"

"For bravery, maybe," Tina suggested.

A hot flush crept up my cheeks. "I didn't do

anything brave," I tried to explain. "Brave is when you make a choice to do something scary. Man, no way would I ever *choose* kidney disease!"

It was wonderful to see everyone again, to feel so appreciated. But the big welcome was starting to make me uneasy. I stood at center stage, and I was supposed to play the role of the hero. It wasn't a part I had auditioned for, and it didn't belong to me.

After a while, though, people would begin to forget. The days and weeks would pile up, putting my illness and CAPD farther and farther behind me. I would fade back into the main company, and if I stepped into the spotlight again it would be by my own choice.

Time would take care of everything. Good old time!

Dr. Wong and the surgeon didn't want me to do much stretching and leaping until my stitches were completely healed, so I couldn't go back to ballet until the end of the summer. I took it slowly at first. Miss Panova told me not to push myself, to begin with the basics and work my way back. My body had stiffened up all over again, but I wasn't worried. It was just one more problem that time would cure — time, and a whole lot of exercise.

Some days I thought I would never get used to feeling so well. In the mornings I sprang awake, as though it were Christmas. Free from tubes and plastic bags of dialysis solution, I leapt out of bed and into my clothes. It was fun to sprint for the bus, my body light and quick and responsive to my every command. Even starting high school seemed like a glorious adventure. The place was so big, so full of possibilities. There was so much to learn. There were so many interesting new people to meet.

Sometimes after school I hung out with Lici. We worked on ballet exercises, or watched videos and enjoyed the chaos of aunts and uncles and cousins and sisters. I had other friends at school now, too. Sometimes I ate lunch with Melanie. She wasn't at all quiet, really, once she got to know you. But she still had a way of announcing what I was going to do — and I still had a tendency not to argue with her.

It was Melanie who informed me that I ought to drop by the local branch library for an exhibit of work by Chicago artists. We both went, and after I wandered around for a while looking at some pretty mind-boggling abstracts, I saw a notice about a free painting class. It was held Saturday mornings, so it didn't conflict with my ballet schedule. I wrote about it in my next letter to Vera. *I don't know if I'll ever enjoy art as much as dancing*, I told her, *but it's a lot of fun dabbing paint on paper*.

At first I wrote to Vera almost every week. I

enclosed little presents I hoped she would like — a Garfield comic strip, a poem I copied out of our English lit book, or one of my drawings. Writing those letters reminded me of the days when I used to keep my secret diary. I wanted to share everything that happened to me, all of the pieces of my day. I wrote about math tests and book reports, fights with Phoebe and trips to the store.

Vera didn't write as often, and her letters were thinner than mine. I knew she was busy, between her work and Brent, so I tried not to be disappointed. I couldn't really expect her to care if a bunch of boys cut into the cafeteria line ahead of me, or to be very excited because Mom said we could keep the black-and-white kitten Phoebe found. After a few weeks, I began to think my letters must seem rather childish to her. Besides, I was pretty busy myself. I didn't really have time to fill up page after page with trivia.

Somehow time speeded up, and I couldn't keep track of the days. Suddenly one morning I realized that in only two more weeks Vera would be back in Chicago. I dug out her last letter to make sure. *I'll be tied up with the convention at McCormick Place most of the time,* she wrote, *but I'd love to see you. Maybe we could have dinner at my hotel Saturday night.*

How could I have forgotten that she was coming so soon? When we said good-bye back at the hospital, I felt lost and empty, as if part of myself were going away. If it hadn't been for her, I'd still be living in that in-between place, not exactly sick but certainly not well, my day cut into little segments between sessions with those tubes and bags.

I studied the calendar in the kitchen, and drew a circle around Saturday the 19th. There weren't many pages left. Another year was drawing to a close. It was hard to believe I was the same person who got sick with HSP little more than twelve months ago. I felt so much older, like someone different.

I would make Vera a present, I decided. I'd draw her a picture. No, I had sent her drawings before, that wouldn't seem very special. Maybe I could write a poem, just for her. The only problem was that my attempts at poetry always got stuck after the second line. What I had to say to Vera wouldn't come out very clearly in words, anyway.

I went upstairs and attacked my homework. I had about twenty-five algebra equations to do, but my mind kept drifting back to Vera's present. It wouldn't be right to go to the mall and buy her some perfume. I wanted to give her something meaningful, something that reflected who I was and let her see the life she had restored to me.

I paced around the room, touching my bronze ballerina figurine, my owl bookends, my good-luck peacock feather. They were all fragments of my personal history, but none of them could speak the message I wanted to send.

Then I remembered the scrapbook, buried on the top shelf of my closet. I had big plans for organizing my ballet pictures when I got it for my twelfth birthday, but somehow I never found the time. On the first page was a photograph of me in a frilly costume from my first-year recital, and a copy of the programme. But the rest was still blank. I could use it for anything I liked.

I found a lot of old photos in a box under my bed. But most of them didn't go back very far, only to fourth or fifth grade. Mom had earlier ones somewhere, shots of our old house, of me on the slide at nursery school, even a few toothless grinning baby pictures. And someplace we must still have a copy of that old newspaper article with a picture of me shaking hands with the mayor. They had run a big story after my second-grade class collected aluminum cans for Earth Day.

"Rachel," Mom called outside my door. "Aren't you done with your homework yet? It's ten-thirty!"

"Not quite," I said. "Hey, you remember that time I was in the paper? We've still got that article, don't we?"

Mom peered in at me, frowning. "I haven't seen it around in years. How much more work do you have? You've got to get to bed."

"Not that much," I said. "Wasn't there a box we packed a lot of old papers and stuff in when we moved?"

"Oh, it's around," Mom said. "Don't stay up half the night. Get your homework done and go to sleep."

"Come on, I'm in high school now," I began, but it was no use arguing. "Okay, I will." I sighed. Sometimes it was tough enough to deal with just one mother, let alone two!

# 18

Chip and I went to the same high school, but the place was so huge I hardly expected to run into him. Then one day at lunch, as I maneuvered toward a half-filled table in the corner, a voice called, "Peanut butter!"

I was so startled I nearly dropped my tray. But I regained my balance in time to smile over at Chip and answer, "Jelly!"

"We can't go on like this," he said, as though he were on an afternoon soap opera. "I have to tell you the truth. I don't remember your name. Whenever I look at you, all I can think of is 'Smooth or Crunchy?'"

For a second I felt stung. We had worked on the yearbook together for months. I thought we knew each other pretty well. How could he forget me so quickly?

Then I caught his grin. It was all part of his act, something he said to get a laugh. He really did look comical, a short, determined figure staggering under a tray so full of food it could topple him onto the floor. I did laugh, just as he wanted me to.

We grabbed two seats at a table full of sophomores, and Chip filled me in on his year so far. "The coach begged me to go out for basketball," he explained, with almost a straight face. "I had to tell him no — there are so many other guys who deserve the chance, it wouldn't be fair to them." Then he turned serious. "Actually, I joined the Mummers Society. You know, that's the drama club."

"Are you going to be in a play?" I asked eagerly. It would take guts to get out on stage in that huge auditorium. You'd face an audience of hundreds — no, thousands of people!

"I tried out for *Arsenic and Old Lace*," he said. "I wanted to be the mad brother who thinks he's digging the Panama Canal in the cellar. But I didn't get the part."

"Oh," I said. "That's a bummer, after you got your hopes up."

Chip shrugged. "Freshmen hardly ever make it. I'll still work on sets and costumes, and I'll get to see the show from the audience instead of sitting backstage." He paused and eyed me thoughtfully. "I've got an extra ticket for Saturday night," he said, and I never imagined he could sound so shy. "You doing anything? You — could you — would you like to go?"

I guess I was a little slow. It took me a moment to grasp what he was saying. Chip was inviting me out, for a real genuine date! My first date since Mario Minutelli asked me to the sock hop in seventh grade. "Sure," I said. "That'd be — " I stopped short. "Saturday the nineteenth?"

"Yeah. What's the matter?"

How was I going to explain this one? Sorry I can't go out with you, I've got a big date with my mother? For a moment I wished I didn't have to see Vera at all — but only for a moment. I was looking forward to seeing her. I was practically counting the days. Wasn't I?

"I've got to go somewhere that night," I said. "Someone's coming in from California — somebody I don't get to see all that often."

"Oh." Chip looked gloomily at his plate of lasagna. But in a moment he brightened again. "Well, maybe another time. You can come see me when I'm a star."

"Sure," I said. "I'll clap. I'll throw flowers."

I hoped Chip wouldn't be discouraged, now that I had turned him down. But I had the feeling I didn't need to worry. He was the sort of guy who didn't discourage easily.

My scrapbook for Vera was nearly finished when Mom finally found that newspaper clipping with me and the mayor. I had forgotten that I had two front teeth missing in the picture. There

I was, with a big gap right in the middle of my smile. My hair was flying all over, too, as if I'd just spent half an hour under an electric fan. "Well, I hope Vera won't mind the natural me," I said, tucking it carefully away.

"Can I see what else you've got there?" Mom asked.

I handed her the book, and she turned carefully from page to page, studying each picture and memento. I had tried to start as early as I could, with a couple of baby pictures, and a shot of the first house we ever lived in, with a big old oak tree in front. I'd glued in a starfish I found on Cape Cod, and a picture of Vicki, who was my best friend until we moved to Chicago. There was even a photograph of me at about four, hanging onto a chair as I tried to do a *plié*. Mom always said I was excited about ballet when I was little, but I hadn't known she meant *that* little.

I watched Mom's face, trying to read her reaction. She was so strange about Vera when we were in the hospital together, and afterward she tended to get quiet and tense when I brought up her name. She'd been a little better lately, though. But perhaps that was because I didn't talk about Vera quite so often.

"I bet she'll love it," Mom said, handing back the scrapbook. "I forgot we'd saved that story you wrote in first grade, the one about 'The Elafunt and the Jeraf.' "

"You don't think it was dumb to stick that in?"

"No, of course not. Mothers get a kick out of things like that."

A weight lifted from my chest and floated silently away. Mom wasn't afraid of Vera anymore, or jealous of her either. For the first time she had simply referred to the fact that Vera was my mother, too, that she too might get silly and sentimental over some half-scrawled, misspelled story by six-year-old me. I could write to Vera, and give her my scrapbook, and see her when she came to Chicago without making Mom unhappy.

"Wait a minute," Mom said. "I think I've got something you can give to her."

She disappeared down the hall, and in a moment she was back, carrying a framed photograph. It was a baby picture in a round silver frame. I sat in a pile of sand, smiling so much you could almost hear me laugh. That picture had stood on Mom's dresser for as long as I could remember.

"You're sure you want to give it away?" I asked, taking it gingerly.

Mom nodded. "It's hardly a fair trade," she said. "We give her a picture. She gave us you."

I'd never taken the El downtown by myself before, but Vera was going to be busy at the convention all day, so she didn't have time to pick me up. I felt years older, charting out my journey from Monroe Street, where I'd get off the train, to the Palmer House, where Vera was staying. The Palmer House was one of the fanciest hotels in the city, and Vera said we could eat at one of the restaurants there. You couldn't design a more grown-up occasion than that.

But as I headed for the front door, Mom reminded me that I was still just a kid. "Hang onto your purse," she cautioned. "Don't just let it swing free like an invitation."

I hugged my purse like a teddy bear and reached for the doorknob.

"Don't talk to any strangers," she added. "Call us if you run into trouble."

"I won't," I said. "I will." And at last I was on my way.

The train filled up as we roared closer to the Loop. I tuned in on a conversation between a skinny bearded guy and his girlfriend, who had bright orange hair and hoop earrings dangling to her shoulders. "I didn't sleep a minute last night," she said breathlessly. "I can't stand this! What if you get caught?"

The train screeched around a bend, and I missed his reply. When we rolled into the next station he was saying, ". . . just forget it. Forget it. Forget it ever happened. Let's talk about something else."

Maybe his pockets bulged with stolen diamonds. Maybe he was on his way to throw a murder weapon into the lake. I tried to memorize his face, so I could recognize it on the news tomorrow.

I was so busy thinking about secret crimes that I nearly missed my stop. And I was out on the sidewalk before I thought of Vera again. Somehow, the scrapbook, which weighed down my purse, began to seem like a bad idea. Maybe she would think I was totally self-centered, giving her all those pictures of myself as if they were some royal legacy. Perfume or bubble bath would have been a safer bet.

I felt very alone as I hurried along the crowded street, clutching my purse against my side. When a man stepped out of a doorway and asked me the time, I strode past him without a word. Mom's warnings echoed in my head. Hang onto your purse . . . don't talk to strangers . . .

The revolving door of the Palmer House swept me from one world into another. The raucous street disappeared, and the hotel lobby engulfed me in its quiet elegance. The walls and ceilings were adorned with classical Greek paintings — nymphs and griffins and winged gods. Golden cherubs played around the face of a great carved clock.

Most of the men I saw wore suits, and a couple of the women had on long evening dresses. I searched the unfamiliar faces for Vera, but she was not here. Any moment now, someone would ask me if I were lost. With every passing second,

I grew more convinced that I was.

Timidly, almost on tiptoe, I approached the reception desk. I'd wait five minutes, then ask if anyone had left a message for me. Vera had called just last Sunday to get the details straight, I reminded myself. She certainly wouldn't forget.

"Rachel!"

I spun around, dizzy with relief. Vera hurried toward me. Her face was flushed, as though she had run all the way from the convention center. "Sorry to keep you waiting!" she exclaimed. "It all took longer than I expected over there. I had to take down most of our exhibit and lock everything into a cabinet — anything that isn't bolted down walks away. I'm starving, how about you?"

"Kind of," I said. I trailed after her across the lobby and down carpeted stairs. A dull, let-down feeling tugged at me. Wasn't Vera excited to see me again? She was in such a hurry we hardly had a chance to greet each other. All she could talk about were her exhibits and her appetite.

We both relaxed once we were seated at the restaurant. It was called Trader Vic's, and the decor was South Seas, with pictures of beaches and palm trees, and a huge outrigger canoe hanging from the ceiling. Even the tables were carved to look like chunks of driftwood. "Well," Vera said with a long, appraising glance, "how are you?"

After what I'd been through over the past year, "how are you" would never be a casual question again. "I feel fine," I said. "I really do. Everything's been going great so far!"

"You look terrific," Vera said. "Nice and slim, good color in your cheeks."

"Hey, I *must* be feeling better!" I said, laughing. "This is the first time I've thought about my body all day! According to Miss Lundy, that's the sign of genuine health."

I had told so many stories in my letters that I thought Vera would recognize Miss Lundy's name. But she asked, "Who's that?" and I got that let-down feeling again.

We pored over the menu, and Vera recommended a dish with chicken and rice, pineapple and coconut milk. The waiter brought us drinks — some sort of rum concoction for Vera, and a ginger ale for me. A lemon slice perched on the rim of my glass, so it looked like a cocktail instead of pop.

Maybe this would be a good time to give her the presents, I decided. But just as I reached for my purse, our waiter was back with a plate of butterfly shrimp. Soon the table was littered with dishes and silverware, and it would have been awkward for her to open packages in the middle of the feast.

The dinner was delicious. I really appreciated food now, after having been deprived for so long.

Still, after the first few bites, I noticed that neither of us was talking.

"What's the convention like?" I asked, to fill up the silence.

"It's an enormous room with row after row of booths — all displaying educational toys. Everything from chemistry sets to puzzle maps to life-sized models. Hundreds of computer games. You can't imagine the stuff that's over there!"

"Phoebe'd love it," I said. "I probably would, too."

"I've been thinking about that mobile space unit Phoebe wanted to invent," Vera said. "I tossed out the idea to one of our engineers. He's making a couple of sketches."

"Wow! They might actually build it?"

"Well, maybe. But they make sketches of lots of things."

The silence settled around us again. I asked her how Brent was, and she said he was just fine. This summer they might go to Hawaii.

Somewhere in the back of my mind I had kept a secret fantasy, a picture of Vera and me racing through summer on a California beach. Now, with barely a whimper, my California dream withered and died. Even if Vera were going to be around this summer, what would I do out there anyway? She'd be busy every day, between her work and being a newlywed. I'd be on my own, with nothing to do.

"Did you ever see *Arsenic and Old Lace?*" I asked suddenly.

Vera shook her head. "No. Why?"

"Nothing. I was just thinking . . ." I wondered if Chip had asked someone else to go with him. It was supposed to be a fantastic production — the acting, the sets, everything about it. The next time the Mummers did a show, I wouldn't miss it. The next time Chip asked me out, I'd say yes.

At last the waiter cleared away the remnants of our dinner. Vera and I sat opposite each other across the empty table. It was time. "I brought you something," I said, and drew out my package.

The wrapping paper was a bit crumpled, after being stuffed into my pocketbook. But Vera admired the package for a good long moment, as if it had been gift-wrapped at Marshall Field's.

Slowly, carefully, she pulled the paper away. "O-oh!" she murmured, lifting the cover. "Oh, Rachel! This is wonderful!"

She didn't speak as she turned through the pages, pausing now and then to study one picture or another, then moving on again. When she finally looked up, her eyes glistened with tears.

I turned away, a little embarrassed. "There's something else," I told her. "My mom sent you this."

Reverently, Vera turned the picture in her hands, as though it were a jewel. "That's so kind

182

of her," she exclaimed. "Does she really want to give this away?"

"She wants you to have it," I said.

We had chosen well. Our gifts were perfect. I could never fully repay Vera, but I had found a way to give her something that had real meaning.

And now it was done. Our questions were answered, hers and mine. Fate had flung us together, and we had exchanged gifts. I knew that Vera's to me was greater than anything I could give in return. Yet I had given her something she needed. She knew now that she had made the right decision all those years ago. As her life unfolded before her, she could be at peace with what she had done.

Mom wasn't jealous of Vera anymore. She knew, even before I knew myself, that I was ready to let Vera go. I *had* a mother already. I had a family, a world to live in. Vera would not be with me as my life flowed toward the future. She would be across the continent, in a life of her own.

The waiter brought the check. "I thought maybe we'd have time to see a movie tonight," Vera told me. "But it's getting late — and I have some calls to make. Would you mind — "

"No," I said. "It's okay."

"Maybe next time I'm in town," she went on apologetically as we made our way back to the lobby. "I do so much traveling, I know I'll hit Chicago again before too long."

Vera waited with me as the doorman found me a taxi. I had never taken one by myself, but Mom had insisted that the El wasn't safe after dark. Would the driver be quiet or talkative, I wondered. Was I supposed to speak to him? He'd be a stranger, after all.

"I'll send you some of our wedding pictures," Vera promised.

"I'll write to you," I told her. And I knew I would — now and then, for a while.

"Let me know when you have your next recital," Vera said. "Oh, look — there's your cab!"

She held out her arms, and I ran to her for a quick, parting hug. Then I was out on the sidewalk, scrambling into the backseat of the taxi.

"Where to?" the driver asked, pulling into the traffic.

I twisted in my seat to peer through the rear window. Vera stood at the curb, watching me out of sight. She caught my eye and waved. I waved back, and saw her smile. Then a lumbering van got in the way, and I couldn't see her any longer.

"You didn't hear me or what?" the driver snapped. "I says where you going to?"

I waved once more, toward the place where I thought Vera might still be standing. Then I turned to face forward. "Home," I said, and gave him my address.

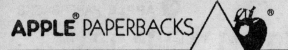

## APPLE® PAPERBACKS

# *Pick an Apple and Polish Off Some Great Reading!*

## BEST-SELLING APPLE TITLES

| | | |
|---|---|---|
| ❏ MT43944-8 | **Afternoon of the Elves** Janet Taylor Lisle | $2.75 |
| ❏ MT43109-9 | **Boys Are Yucko** Anna Grossnickle Hines | $2.75 |
| ❏ MT43473-X | **The Broccoli Tapes** Jan Slepian | $2.95 |
| ❏ MT42709-1 | **Christina's Ghost** Betty Ren Wright | $2.75 |
| ❏ MT43461-6 | **The Dollhouse Murders** Betty Ren Wright | $2.75 |
| ❏ MT43444-6 | **Ghosts Beneath Our Feet** Betty Ren Wright | $2.75 |
| ❏ MT44351-8 | **Help! I'm a Prisoner in the Library** Eth Clifford | $2.75 |
| ❏ MT44567-7 | **Leah's Song** Eth Clifford | $2.75 |
| ❏ MT43618-X | **Me and Katie (The Pest)** Ann M. Martin | $2.75 |
| ❏ MT41529-8 | **My Sister, The Creep** Candice F. Ransom | $2.75 |
| ❏ MT42883-7 | **Sixth Grade Can Really Kill You** Barthe DeClements | $2.75 |
| ❏ MT40409-1 | **Sixth Grade Secrets** Louis Sachar | $2.75 |
| ❏ MT42882-9 | **Sixth Grade Sleepover** Eve Bunting | $2.75 |
| ❏ MT41732-0 | **Too Many Murphys** Colleen O'Shaughnessy McKenna | $2.75 |

**Available wherever you buy books, or use this order form.**

- - - - - - - - - - - - - - - - - - - - - - - - - - - - - - - - - - - - - - - - - -

**Scholastic Inc., P.O. Box 7502, 2931 East McCarty Street, Jefferson City, MO 65102**

Please send me the books I have checked above. I am enclosing $_____ (please add $2.00 to cover shipping and handling). Send check or money order — no cash or C.O.D.s please.

Name _____

Address _____

City_____ State/Zip _____

Please allow four to six weeks for delivery. Offer good in the U.S.A. only. Sorry, mail orders are not available to residents of Canada. Prices subject to change.

APP591

**6 APPLE**®PACKBACKS

# ADVENTURE! MYSTERY! ACTION!

## Exciting stories for you!